AN ALMOST PE

Fifteen-year-old Ellen Jane Gardner thought she was in for a perfect summer once she landed the job of mother's helper on Cape Cod. She knew the job description didn't specify sunny days at the beach, clam digging with two adorable children, and strolling in the moonlight with a handsome boy, but she fantasized that's what her summer would be like. Even before she's met the Winner family, she thinks her fantasy might come true when she meets gorgeous Todd Crowley, who lives next door to her new employers.

Then Ellen meets Marcie, a ten-year-old spoiled brat who's disposed of eighteen mother's helpers already, and Derek, a five-year-old who doesn't yet talk. Things seem pretty grim when Lisa, the phantom sixteen-year-old sister whom no one bothered to mention in the job description, makes Ellen feel uncomfortable. Ellen knows her job isn't going to be easy but she's determined. It takes all of her imagination to match wits with Marcie and Derek and to figure out exactly what Todd Crowley wants. With more surprises in store, will Ellen be able to finish her summer job with a happy ending?

Also by the same author, and available from Lightning:

THE LOVE CYCLE

An Almost Perfect Summer

Rona S. Zable

LIGHTNING BOOKS
Hodder and Stoughton

First published in the USA in
1989 by Bantam Doubleday
Dell Publishing Group, Inc.

*First published in Great Britain
in 1989 by Lightning*

The characters and situations in this book are entirely imaginary and bear no relation to any real person or actual happenings.

British Library C.I.P.

Zable, Rona S.,
An almost perfect summer.
I. Title
813'.54 [F]

ISBN 0-340-51254-7

Printed and bound in Great Britain for Hodder and Stoughton paperbacks, a division of Hodder and Stoughton Ltd., Mill Road, Dunton Green, Sevenoaks, Kent TN13 2YA (Editorial Office: 47 Bedford Square, London WC1B 3DP) by Cox & Wyman Ltd., Reading, Berks. Typeset by Avocet Robinson, Buckingham.

1

''Wake up, Ellen. Ellen? Ellen, Wake up! We're almost there.'' Mom's voice rudely interrupted the daydream I was having:

Ellen smiled, watching her two young charges—Marcella and Derek—as they romped happily on the sandy white beach below the magnificent Winner mansion.

Suddenly, someone grabbed her arm roughly. ''So you're the new mother's helper!'' said the Handsome, Dark-Haired Stranger, eyeing her boldly.

''Ellen,'' Mom said, tugging my arm. ''We're here.''

Well, so much for *that* fantasy!

I sure had been way off. Instead of the towering mansion overlooking the sea, 66 Harbor Road turned out to be a sprawling, white-painted, Cape Cod house on a tree-lined street, with other houses all around. It had a screened-in front porch and striped blue awnings on the windows. There were rosebushes in full bloom on the velvety green lawn.

''Very nice,'' said Mom approvingly. ''The Winners are certainly doing well.''

''You see? Now aren't you glad you let me come?''

My mother opened the car door slowly. "I still think fifteen is too young to be away from home all summer," she said with a little sigh.

"Fifteen and a half," I corrected her. "And wouldn't you rather have me here instead of hanging around the house all summer with nothing to do? Besides," I added, "I'll come back tan and rich."

Mom started to laugh. "Tan, yes. Rich, no."

"Well, rich enough to buy that typewriter." I stood watching as she fiddled with the lock on the car trunk. The house and street were quiet. There was no sign of Marcella and Derek. I kept craning my neck to see if anybody was around. For the hundredth time, I asked Mom, "What do you suppose they'll be like?"

For the hundredth time, she answered, "I don't really know—I've never met Thelma's children. But I'm sure they're lovely. And bright too, I'd imagine. After all, she and Martin are both lawyers and . . ."

Marcella came racing out of the house to greet Ellen. "We're so happy you've come," she cried joyfully. "Here—let me help you with your suitcase." Marcella was a slender child, ten years old, with a reserved, gentle manner.

Her five-year-old brother, Derek, was a spirited, lively chatterbox. "Ellen," he said, "would you—"

"Would you *please* take this suitcase?" Mom was saying.

"Sorry," I apologized. I took the faded tartan suitcase she was holding and scooped up the shopping bag with my radio and tennis racket in it. As we started toward the house, a little old lady stepped out on the front porch and yoo-hooed to us.

She was wearing a yellow pantsuit that flared above her ankles and a bright yellow bow in her hair. And what hair it was—tiny curls the color of orange soda spilling over her head.

A shiver of excitement ran through me. She reminded me of the strange old lady in the gothic novel I had read the day before.

"That must be the housekeeper," I whispered.

"That's the grandmother," Mom whispered back. "And please, honey—no fantasies. This is Cape Cod—not Wuthering Heights."

The little old lady smiled at us as we climbed the porch steps. "Laura, I wouldn't have recognized you," she declared, squinting up at Mom. "You look so nice. How many years has it been? I think it was a Whatchamacallit's wedding, wasn't it?"

The two of them hugged and kissed, chatting for a few minutes about my aunt Mildred and uncle Ben and different people they knew. Then Mom put her arm around me and said, "This, of course, is my daughter, Ellen. Ellen, this is Mrs. Brill, Thelma Winner's mother."

"Just call me Grandma Brill," said the little lady. "Everybody does." She led us into the house, talking away and hopping from one subject to another. "Thelma said she's sorry she couldn't be here but she had to go to court this morning. . . . Goodness, I can't believe how long it's been since I saw you. . . . Who'd expect so much traffic on a Monday! . . . So now that Thelma is in with Martin, the name of their firm is Winner & Winner."

"That's a good name for a law firm," Mom said. "Aunt Mildred tells me Martin is one of the most successful trial lawyers on the Cape."

Grandma gave us a quick tour of the downstairs as Mom ooh-ed and aah-ed. This was not the elegant mansion of my fantasy, but still—compared to our little apartment in Pawtucket, the Winner homestead was House Beautiful.

There was a living room with heavy dark furniture and deep gold carpeting, a formal dining room, a sun porch, a family room and a cozy little den with a big TV set blaring away even though nobody was watching it.

"The children," Grandma Brill sighed, shutting off the set. "They're so wasteful."

"Where *are* the children?" I asked. "I can't wait to meet them."

"They went to do some errands with Whoosis—oh, what's his name anyhow—the boy who takes care of the yard." Grandma shook her orange curls. "Well, anyhow, they should be back in about an hour."

"An hour?" Mom looked at her watch. "Oh, dear, I really can't wait that long. I did want to meet the children, too, but I promised my boss I'd be back in the office."

"Mom, that's okay," I reassured her. "You can meet them some other time. Maybe you should start driving back now, before the traffic gets heavy."

Mom said her good-byes to Grandma Brill, and the two of us walked out to the car. Mom put her arm around me and said, "Now remember, honey. This is a job, a responsibility. It's not just fun and games and lying around the beach all summer long."

I nodded dutifully.

"And please, Ellen," she continued, "Don't mope around daydreaming all the time. You're a mother's helper—not a governess in one of those books you're always reading."

"I'll miss you," she added, hugging me.

From out of nowhere, I felt a prickling sensation in the back of my eyes, as if I were going to start crying.

"I'm going to miss *you*, Mom." It had just ocurred to me that, except for the four days when I had visited my dad and his new wife in Atlanta, I had never been away from home before.

But then I thought about the fabulous summer I was going to have and my heart raced with excitement.

Here I was—Ellen Jane Gardner of Pawtucket, Rhode Island—with a Dream Job any 15-year-old girl would *die* for—mother's helper for two little rich kids on beautiful Cape Cod!

I could see it all now . . .

Long golden days on sandy white beaches . . . pounding surf and fog-shrouded lighthouses . . . picturesque harbors . . . digging for clams with Marcella and Derek . . . walking in the moon-light with Handsome, Dark-haired Stranger . . .

"And don't forget to put sunscreen on your nose, Ellen." Mom leaned out of the car window. I leaned over and kissed her good-bye.

She chugged down Harbor Road, and I stood there watching until I couldn't see the car any more.

It was the oddest sensation. I had a lump in my throat, but I also had this incredible feeling of freedom—of being on my own, with all kinds of exciting new things about to happen.

"Don't forget to put sunscreen on your nose, Ellen," said a deep voice from behind me.

I jumped and spun around, and I couldn't believe what I saw. The voice belonged to a boy who looked as if he had stepped right out of one of my fantasies. He was maybe 17 or 18. And absolutely gorgeous. He was tall, tan and lean-jawed, with dark hair and brown velvet eyes.

"With that cute little nose, you won't need much sunscreen," he said, smiling at me.

My insides were fluttering. I couldn't believe this was actually happening to me. I had always read about moments when time stands still. I felt rooted there, along with the rosebushes. Droplets of spray were hitting me from the lawn sprinkler, but I couldn't move.

"You must be the mother's helper," he said, looking me over.

I could feel my mouth dropping open. *I had daydreamed about this only a little while ago!*

Before I could say a word, Grandma Brill's voice broke the magic. "Yoo-hoo, Ellen," she was calling from the front porch. "Yoo-hoo. Come on in. Your tea is getting cold."

The Handsome, Dark-Haired Stranger grinned and waved to Grandma Brill. "See you later, Ellen," he said softly.

He walked away, and I stumbled up the front stairs, still in a daze. Why, oh why, did Grandma Brill have to interrupt us at that very moment? I know she meant well, but I don't even *like* tea, hot *or* cold!

I followed her into the house, all out of breath. ''Er—do you happen to know—uh—the name of that boy who was talking to me outside?'' I stammered.

''That's—oh, what's his name?'' Grandma smacked her hand against her forehead as if that would help her remember. ''It's on the tip of my . . . I know his name as well as . . .'' She looked like she was about to cry, and I felt guilty for even asking.

I hadn't seen the kitchen before. It was big and modern, done in blue and white. There was a huge butcher-block table in the center of the room, with eight chairs grouped around it.

It was also the messiest kitchen you could imagine, with an overpowering smell of oranges and sour milk. Breakfast dishes were still on the table. Cereal boxes were open, and one had tipped over, sending Cherrios to the floor. The dishwasher yawned open, full of so many dishes, glasses, and pots that it couldn't possibly close. Nearby a brown garbage bag overflowed with squeezed-out oranges.

''Please excuse the mess,'' Grandma said. She had cleared off two places at the table and put out mugs of tea with a plate of oddly shaped cookies.

I took a sip of my tea. It tasted like lukewarm cardboard. I could only imagine how long that tea bag had been sitting in the cup. I put in two extra sugars to disguise the taste.

Suddenly Grandma Brill let out a loud shriek.

''Todd! It's Todd!'' she yelled wildly. ''That's it—Todd Crowley!''

I was so startled I almost spilled my tea.

''See—didn't I tell you it was on the tip of my

tongue?'' she said happily. ''That's his name—the boy you were talking to before. He lives next door in the gray house.''

''*He lives next door*?'' I repeated, incredulous. This time the tea went down the wrong way, and I started to cough and choke.

Grandma rushed over to me and pulled my arms above my head. ''Keep looking up,'' she cried, ''That's it—look up at the birdie. You'll be all right.''

We heard the crunch of tires in the driveway. ''That sounds like the children,'' Grandma Brill said. The screen door banged.

''Well, look who's here,'' she said, her face beaming, ''our little sweethearts.''

In came the most adorable child I'd ever seen. He had chestnut-brown curls, rosy cheeks, and merry brown eyes. One finger was stuffed into his mouth and he clutched a lacy pink nightgown.

''Derek, this is your new mother's helper,'' Grandma Brill said, bending down to him. ''Can you say hello to Ellen?''

Perfect, I thought to myself, *just perfect*. It was as if little Derek had stepped right out of my fantasy.

Grandma Brill kept coaxing him to say something. But Derek just stood there, staring first at her, then at me, not saying a word.

''What's the matter?'' Grandma teased him playfully. ''Cat got your tongue?''

As soon as she said that, Derek began to cry. He ran off, sobbing loudly, the pink nightgown trailing behind him like a bridal train.

''Oh, goodness,'' Grandma said, covering her mouth with her hand. ''I keep forgetting I should never say that to Derek. It frightens him when people talk about a cat getting his tongue.''

She mulled over that thought for a moment and continued. ''Maybe that's why Derek doesn't like cats. Then again, maybe that's why he's afraid to talk. And then again, maybe he's afraid if he did start to talk, a cat would jump up and get his tongue. I don't know *what* to think.''

She stared at me helplessly, as if she expected me to have the answer.

In between sighs, Grandma told me that little Derek hardly spoke at all. Maybe about four or five words. Not exactly an impressive vocabulary for a five-year-old, to say the least. ''But the doctor says there's nothing wrong with him,'' she explained. ''He understands everything.'' Another huge sigh. ''My daughter Thelma says Derek is probably just a late bloomer.''

Poor kid, I thought. I couldn't help feeling a stab of disappointment that Derek wasn't the lively, talkative little boy I had pictured he would be. I had imagined writing letters back home about all the cute and clever things Derek had said.

Oh, well, there was always Marcella. She would be like a little sister to me. We would go swimming, play tennis, have wonderful heart-to-heart talks. She and I would bake cookies together, and I would make a French braid in her long golden hair. A scene flashed before me:

The kitchen gleamed invitingly as Ellen placed a vase of freshly picked roses on the scrubbed butcher-block table.

Marcella entered shyly, brown as a berry from romping outdoors.

"Oh, Ellen," she cried happily, "you cleaned up the kitchen. How lovely you have made our home . . ."

THWOCK—THWOCK—THWOCK!

Something smacked me on the side of my head.

"Another country heard from," Grandma Brill sighed heavily, putting down her cup of tea.

I whirled around. There stood a fat little girl in a gray jogging suit. She had short, frizzy brown hair and pale skin. From behind pink-rimmed glasses, her little eyes glittered.

She picked up the pink rubber ball that had hit me. My left ear was still smarting from it.

THWOCK—THWOCK—THWOCK. She bounced the ball on the kitchen floor, scattering the spilled Cheerios every which way.

"Who's *she*?" the girl asked, jutting her chin at me.

"That's Ellen—the new Mother's Helper," Grandma Brill said. "And Marcie, please don't bounce—"

THWOCK—THWOCK—THWOCK. The ball landed inside one of the orange rinds sitting atop the garbage bag. The little girl looked at me and said, "Well, if you're a mother's helper, help get that ball."

Grandma Brill jumped up and pulled the ball out of the orange rind, wiping it off with a napkin left over from breakfast.

What a rude little girl, I thought indignantly. How could Marcella even *associate* with someone like that?

She grabbed the ball. Then she stamped her foot and yelled, "How many times do I have to tell everybody—*we don't want a mother's helper!*''

Suddenly I got a quivery, sinking kind of feeling, as if somebody had emptied an ice cube tray around my heart.

Grandma Brill patted the little yellow bow in her hair. In a small, nervous, voice she said, ''Ellen, this is my granddaughter, Marcie.''

2

Things were certainly not going the way Bobbie-Lou and I had figured.

Bobbie-Lou Womack is my best friend back home in Pawtucket. Everyone is kind of surprised when they find out Bobbie is her real name—it's not Roberta or anything like that. Bobbie's mother comes from the South, which is why she likes those double names.

Anyhow, Bobbie-Lou likes to read romance novels as much as I do, and we both have pretty active imaginations. When I learned I had gotten this job, the two of us talked for hours, thinking up all these terrific fantasies about my summer on Cape Cod.

Only we had pictured it differently—like with me being a sort of teenage Mary Poppins and with Marcella and Derek overjoyed to have me there.

Somehow it had never occurred to either Bobbie-Lou or me that Marcella would turn out to be Marcie. And Mega-Brat Marcie, at that.

Also we hadn't figured that Derek would be traveling in the slow lane either.

Oh, well, I consoled myself. At least part of the fanatasy we dreamed up had come true: I had met the Handsome, Dark-Haired Stranger. And to think Todd Crowley lived right next door!

Grandma Brill helped me carry my things upstairs. Marcie followed us, but she didn't even offer to help. Instead she walked right behind me up the stairs, stepping on my heels.

My room was small but pretty, done in yellow dotted swiss with a ruffled canopy over the bed. On the shelves above the white-and-gold desk was a huge doll collection that seemed to be staring right at me.

Grandma Brill was rattling the hangers in the closet as I put my suitcases down, looking around. ''This is nice,'' I said.

''It ought to be nice,'' Marcie snapped. ''It's *my* bedroom. And I had to give it up just so a dumb mother's helpless could have it.''

So that was why Marcie was the way she was. She'd had to give up her bedroom. ''Oh, gee, I'm sorry—I didn't realize this—'' I started to say, but she cut me short.

''And I'm warning you—don't make a mess of this room!'' That was her final comment as she clumped off downstairs. All the while, Grandma Brill had stayed inside the closet, making believe she was doing something with the hangers. I had a hunch she was a little afraid of Marcie and that's why she didn't discipline her.

I finished unpacking, freshened up and then headed down to the kitchen. Earlier, when I'd been having tea with Grandma Brill, I had offered to clean up the kitchen. I figured that would show them how responsible and hardworking I was. Grandma had accepted my offer with pleasure. She had also asked if I would mind if she went off to her senior citizens' meeting. ''I'll only be gone a couple of hours or so. Do you think you'll be all right alone here?''

''Oh, sure,'' I had told her. ''You just go ahead.

I'll straighten up and fix lunch for the children."

As I washed the breakfast dishes, I gazed out the kitchen window. A tall boy with red hair was clipping hedges in the yard. Next to him stood Marcie, and I could hear her laughing. Derek was happily digging in a patch of dirt with a big soup ladle.

Just then the telephone rang. "Is Lisa there?" a girl's voice demanded.

"Sorry," I told her, "there's nobody here named Lisa. You must have the wrong number."

A few seconds later, the phone rang again. It was the same girl calling. I recognized her voice right away. She had one of those snobby boarding school accents, and she sounded quite annoyed.

By the third call, she sounded furious. "Is this some kind of stupid joke? What number is this?"

I looked down to read off the telephone number, but it had been scribbled over with Magic Marker. "Uh—I don't know," I said.

"You don't even know your phone number?" The voice sounded incredulous. "Everybody knows their phone number."

"Well, um, this isn't my phone. I mean, I don't live here. I'm the new mother's helper and—"

"Oh, cripes, I might have known." She sounded disgusted. "Another one. This must be the Winner house, right? Listen—tell Lisa to call Brandy—it's important." With that she clicked off.

I knew there was nobody in the house named Lisa, but I figured I ought to write down the message anyhow. Maybe Lisa was a neighbor or a relative. I had started to pull off a piece of paper towel to write the message down when Marcie stomped into the kitchen.

"Me and Derek could starve to death," she

complained. "It's lunchtime, ya know."

"Wow—time sure flies when you're having fun," I joked, but Marcie just glared at me.

"Make me a sardine and tomato sandwich on white bread with butter. And don't squash those sardines, either. Derek doesn't want anything right now." She marched out, slamming the back door, and then reappeared. "And I want a grape soda with ice in it."

"You're welcome," I said, but she was already gone.

I hunted for a can of sardines on the cluttered shelves, thinking about my Game Plan. Marcie's not all that bad, I told myself. Once she gets used to me, she'll be fine. In a day or two, we'll probably be great friends. Anyhow, I couldn't feel too upset about Marcie, since I was still so thrilled about meeting Todd Crowley and finding out he lived right next door.

I started to wind the key on the sardine can, but it only would go in a little way. No matter how I tried to twist it, the key wouldn't budge. I finally gave up and dug out the sardines with a knife.

Marcie noticed, of course. When I brought her sandwich outside, she lifted the top slice of bread and made a face. "I knew it—you squished the sardines. This tastes like sardine soup."

Again I tried to make a joke. "Think of it as a kind of sardine paté," I said, but she just gave a sound of disgust. She did, however, finish every bite of the sandwich.

I looked around the yard, with its beautiful profusion of rosebushes, manicured hedges and flower beds. What a gorgeous day to be outside.

I decided to stay in the yard and get better acquainted with Marcie and Derek, since I'd just about finished cleaning the kitchen.

I pulled over a lawn chair and sat down next to Marcie. She shot me a dirty look. "What are you hanging around here for? Why don't you go back inside and do some ironing or something."

From the rosebushes on the side of the house, the red-haired yard boy called out, "Marcie, give the girl a break. Don't be so mean."

"I'm not mean," Marcie giggled. By the tone of her giggle, I could tell she had a crush on this teenage gardener.

He walked over to Marcie and gave her a make-believe punch to the jaw. She giggled some more.

"Hello there," he smiled at me. "I'm Pete McIntyre."

The bright noonday sun gleamed off Pete's red hair. Maybe it's an awful thing to say, but I have this thing about people with red hair, especially guys. It's not my fault either. Bobbie-Lou brainwashed me. She always claimed people with red hair have mean tempers and bad breath, especially if they have a lot of freckles. And guys with red hair just aren't sexy, according to Bobbie-Lou.

Still and all, Pete seemed like a nice guy. I smiled back and said, "Hi—I'm Ellen Gardner from Pawtucket, Rhode Island."

Pete whistled. "Rhode Island, huh? Hey, Marcie, your mother must have used up the supply in Massachusetts. Now she has to start importing mother's helpers."

Something about the way Pete used the plural of mother's helper made me uneasy. "What do you mean?'' I asked him, hoping he didn't mean what I thought.

''We already had two girls before you came,'' Marcie informed me, sounding very proud. ''They were college girls. Michelle was the first one, and then there was Jill.''

''And how many girls last summer?'' Pete asked Marcie. ''And the summer before that? Your mother ought to install a revolving front door on this house.''

My mouth felt dry. ''How come they all quit?'' I asked.

Marcie didn't answer. Lost in happy recollection, she said, ''What a wimp Jill was. I called her Jill the Pill. But at least,'' Marcie added, her little eyes looking me over, ''at least *Jill* had nice clothes. Your clothes are *nowhere*, and I *hate* the way your hair just hangs down that way.''

Now, that really got to me. I was about to tell Marcie a thing or two about how she hurt people's feeings, when Pete came to my rescue.

''Well, *I* like the way Ellen looks,'' he said, walking around me slowly and looking me up and down. ''Aha—vot haff ve here?'' Pete started talking in one of those mad European scientist accents. ''Long dark hair—yes, I like dot.'' He peered into my eyes. ''Iss nice color eyes on dot girl. Like green olives. Und a cute figure. I like a girl mit a little meat on der bones.''

I burst out laughing. ''Und a cute smile, too,'' Pete added.

All the while, Marcie sat there scowling. I could tell she was angry because Peter was joking around with me. In a loud voice, she announced: ''This is so, so boring. I am so bored.''

That's it! *Marcie doesn't want to just sit around*

doing nothing, I thought to myself. She wants a mother's helper to do things with.

"Let's do something," I suggested. "What do you feel like doing, Marcie?"

"Well, how should *I* know? You're the mother's helper—*you* think of what to do."

I had noticed the badminton net on the other side of the yard. "Want to play a game of badminton?"

"Ugh. I hate that stupid game."

"Okay, then. Do you want to go for a walk?"

"A walk?" Marcie rolled her eyes upward. "In this heat? I hate walking and getting all sweaty." It turned out she hated just about everything—riding a bicycle, all sports, and exercise of any kind.

I racked my brain. This was truly a challenge. "Then what do you like to do when your friends come over?" I asked.

"I hate my friends," Marcie declared. "Except for Bobby Brain, and he's at computer camp all summer."

"Suppose Bobby Brain wasn't at camp and he came over today," I persisted. "What would you guys do?"

Marcie considered that. "Me and Bobby would play telephone tricks on people," she said.

I collected my thoughts. Inside the house, the telephone was ringing. I started to get up to answer it, but Marcie said, "Don't bother—it's probably just one of Lisa's dumb friends."

My ears perked up. "Did you say *Lisa*? Who's Lisa?" I asked.

"Lisa is my sister, stupid."

Mouth open, I stared at Marcie. "Your sister? I didn't even know you *had* a sister. Where does she live?"

"Where do you suppose a sixteen-year-old girl would live?" Marcie snorted. "Right here, pea brain."

Now I was totally confused. "But your mother never mentioned an older sister. She told me there were only two kids—you and Derek."

"Hah," Marcie snorted. "My mother does that on purpose."

"On purpose? Why?"

"Because," Marcie said, "if a mother's helper heard there's three kids in the family, she'd want more money. And she'd wonder how come Lisa doesn't stay with us."

"Well, how come she doesn't?"

"How *come*?" Marcie's voice rose in anger. "Because Lisa is the princess around *this* house. Everyone spoils her rotten. She never has to do a thing except spend money."

From the pocket of her snug-fitting sweat pants, Marcie pulled out a yellow package of M & M's, popping them into her mouth as she spoke. "You know what I think? I think the *real* reason mother keeps on hiring mother's helpers is for Lisa, not for me and Derek. She wants someone to do Lisa's ironing. My mother says Lisa changes clothes every half hour."

"So that's why your mother asked if I knew how to iron," I blurted out. Suddenly I remembered Thelma Winner's business-like voice calling me from Chatham to discuss what she referred to as "the little nitty-gritty details". One of which happened to be ironing. I had been so anxious to get this job that I'd told her I really liked to iron!

Marcie crumpled up the pack of M & M's and

gave a big yawn. "Anyhow, I don't want to talk about my dumb sister. I'm still bored."

"Maybe tomorrow we could go to the beach," I suggested. "Is it far from here?"

"The beach?" Marcie repeated. There was a silence. Pete stopped clipping. Derek stopped digging.

Finally Marcie spoke. "I *hate* the beach," she said.

I knew she was putting me on. Trying not to smile, I said, "I never heard of a kid your age who hated the beach."

"Well, now you did." Marcie sounded positively happy as she spit out each word. "I hate the sand. I hate the sun. I hate the water. I hate swimming. I *never* go to the beach."

"How can anybody live on Cape Cod and *not* go to the beach?" As I spoke, I noticed Marcie's pale skin. And I knew.

She was telling me the truth. She and Derek obviously didn't go to the beach at all. "And I don't like swimming pools either," Marcie added.

I felt dazed. "Tell me something–if you don't like to go to the beach, where *do* you like to go?"

Marcie thought about that a moment. "I like to go out to eat," she said finally.

What had I gotten myself into? I took a deep breath. "Let me get this straight, Marcie. You don't like any kind of sports, and you don't like going for walks, and you don't like the beach, and you don't like to swim–I mean, *what am I supposed to do with the two of you all summer long*?"

"Hey, that's your problem," Marcie replied. "Why do you think my mother hired you? She doesn't know what to do with us either."

With that, Marcie went over and grabbed Derek's arm, pulling him up roughly. "No more digging," she told him in her bossy voice. "There's a good movie on now. It's about this big monster—you'll like it." Derek dropped his soup ladle and trotted off behind her.

I sank down on the lounge. "Marcie's kidding, isn't she?" I looked at Peter, but he didn't answer.

For some reason, everything struck me funny, and I started to laugh. "And to think my mom was worried that I'd be lying around the beach all day, doing nothing," I said to Pete. "Little did she realize I'd be the only *indoor* mother's helper on Cape Cod."

Pete put down his hedge clippers. "How did you get here in the first place?" he asked.

"It's a long story. My aunt Mildred's husband is a distant relative of someone in Mr. Winner's family," I explained. "Anyhow, Mrs. Winner called Aunt Mildred and asked if she knew any teenage girl who wanted to be a mother's helper. Naturally, my aunt suggested me. The two of us persuaded my mother to let me come."

"And you figured this job would be a piece of cake—summer on Cape Cod and all that, huh?"

"You got it," I sighed. "It was like a dream come true. There aren't many jobs around for fifteen-year-olds, you know."

Peter stared at me thoughtfully. "Marcie is going to try everything to get rid of you," he said. "She's done that to every mother's helper they ever had. She's a tough kid."

"Well, I'm tough, too," I said.

"Nobody ever lasted here longer than a few weeks."

''Well, I'm going to last,'' I said. ''I don't intend to go back to Pawtucket. I *need* this job. I've got my salary spent.''

Pete grinned. ''Oh, yeah? What are you planning to do with those big bucks the Winners are paying you?''

''I'm going to buy an electronic typewriter,'' I answered. For some reason, I found myself telling Pete all about how I wanted to be an author and how I needed to start typing up this book I've been writing. Only two other people in the world know about my book—Mom and Bobbie-Lou.

''Besides,'' I went on, ''with me being away, my mom can save money. She's going to school nights to get her degree, so every little bit helps. And besides all that, there's no point going back home. My best friend, Bobbie-Lou, isn't around. She's in North Carolina for the summer.''

I didn't mention another very important reason I didn't want to leave: Todd Crowley.

''I take it there's not much to do in Pawtucket during the summer,'' Pete said.

''Not unless you're a mosquito,'' I said, and he chuckled.

I picked up Marcie's plate and her glass of grape soda. ''See, the thing is,'' I explained, ''I really wanted to get out of Pawtucket this summer in the worst way.''

''Well,'' Pete said ruefully, ''you sure did, didn't you?''

3

Derek was waiting for me in the kitchen. "Are you hungry?" I asked him. He nodded. "Want a peanut butter sandwich?" Another nod and a smile. I fixed a sandwich for myself, poured two big glasses of milk, and Derek and I ate in companionable silence.

After lunch we joined Marcie in front of the TV set. "This movie sucks," she said, clicking off the set. "That monster isn't even real-looking." I was pleasantly surprised when she asked me to play a game of Monopoly. I was buying my third railroad when the doorbell chimes rang.

"Get that door," Marcie ordered, her mouth full of potato chips. "That's probably my dumb sister Lisa. She always forgets her key." Marcie swept the Monopoly tokens and the money back into the box. "I don't want to play any more," she said. "I'm sick of this game." She didn't fool me. She was mad because I was buying the best property.

The girl standing at the door had her back to me as she waved good-bye to the driver in the silver sports car that had dropped her off. As I unlatched the screen door, a pile of shoe boxes and shopping bags landed on my toes.

A sweet, whispery voice said, "Oh—would you take these packages for me?"

I stared at her, absolutely dumbfounded. Could this be Lisa, sister of Marcie?

Lisa Winner sure wasn't like any sixteen-year-old girl *I* ever knew. Lisa looked like she had stepped out of a Maybelline ad. She was beautiful, and that's a word I have never used to describe anyone. I mean, she was about as perfect as you could get. She had a heart-shaped face, huge brown eyes fringed with thick lashes, creamy skin and long silky hair the color of a Hershey bar. The white sun dress she was wearing showed off her flawless tan and her petite figure.

No wonder Marcie didn't like her. If Lisa had been my sister, I'd have hated her too.

She flopped down on the living room sofa, fanning herself with a shopping bag that said, "Rich Girls Store". In her itty-bitty voice, she told me a sad tale of how the air conditioner had broken down while she was trying on bathing suits. "You can't imagine how awful it was," she said tragically.

Suddenly I remembered that telephone message I had never written down. "You had a phone call—some girl wanted you to call her." For the life of me, I just couldn't remember the girl's name.

"Was it Mandy?" Lisa prompted. That sounded right. "I think so," I said.

"No, it couldn't be Mandy," Lisa frowned prettily. "Mandy's out on the boat today. Was it Tammy? Or Brandy?"

I kept nodding. All the names sounded right. "Which one? Or was it Candace?"

I shook my head in confusion. "Oh, I think it was, um—I'm not really sure . . ."

Lisa was awfully gracious about it. "Well," she

said, "if it's important, I guess they'll call back." To show my gratitude, I carried most of her shopping bags and shoe boxes upstairs.

Lisa's room looked like something out of the Arabian Nights tales. It was huge and expensive-looking, decorated in shades of blue and lavender with the kind of shiny white Oriental-type furniture that costs a fortune. It was also a terrible mess. Half a mess, actually. One part of the room was like a little oasis of neatness, with the bed made and no clothes lying around.

"I have to share this room with my sister, Marcie," Lisa told me with a pitiful sigh. I realized that the neat part of the room belonged to Marcie.

"Just put everything in the closet," Lisa said, waving her hand as if I were a bellhop. I waded through piles of clothes and shoes and forced the closet door open.

There was the muffled sound of ringing somewhere in the room. "Oh, dear," Lisa said, looking around helplessly, "that's my phone. Where *is* that little thing? Do you see it around anywhere?" The two of us looked around, trying to determine where the sound was coming from. Finally Lisa tracked it down. She reached through a pile of clothes and pulled out a pale blue Princess phone. She carried it back to her mirrored dressing table, smiling lovingly at her reflection while she talked.

As I started to leave, she called out to me, "Oh, Miss—oh, *you*—wait a minute." She was gesturing to me, her hand over the receiver. "Oh, listen—would you do me a teensy little favor? Downstairs in the laundry room, there's a clothes basket. If you look inside, there's a pair of pink slacks and . . ."

"And you wondered if I would iron them. Is that it?" I asked.

"That's right," Lisa said in a tone of wonder, like I had ESP or something. "How did you know that? Well, anyhow, as long as you're ironing the slacks, there's this pink and white striped top . . ."

I smiled to myself. In all the time I'd been talking with Lisa and helping carry her packages, never once had she asked my name or who I was.

"By the way, Lisa, my name happens to be Ellen—Ellen Jane Gardner," I called over my shoulder as I marched downstairs to the laundry room. "I'm the new mother's helper."

"Derek seems kind of cranky," Marcie observed when I finally went back into the den after I'd finished ironing Lisa's things. "He has to go take a nap every so often." Derek was whimpering softly and rubbing his eyes. I coaxed him up to his bedroom, where he fell asleep immediately, still clutching his nightgown.

The house was quiet. Grandma Brill was still at her meeting. Lisa was still talking on the telephone and Marcie had settled down to watch some more TV. I asked if she wanted to play another game, but she shook her head. "I want to see this show," she said. "But you don't have to stay inside if you don't want to. As long as Derek's taking a nap, you can go outside in the yard."

I was surprised. Touched, in fact. *I'm starting to win Marcie over*, I told myself happily.

"You probably want to get a tan," she said kindly. How right she was. I didn't want to go back to Pawtucket looking pale.

"Gee, thanks," I said, smiling at her. I ran up

to get my tube of Bain de Soleil, then hurried out to the backyard. Yes indeed, I sure wanted to get every second of sunshine I possibly could—especially if I wasn't going to get to the beach.

But what I really wanted to get was another look at Todd Crowley. Maybe he'd be outside and we could finish the conversation Grandma Brill had interrrupted. I grabbed a chaise lounge and carried it over near the fence that separated the Winner house from Todd's house.

Just my luck. Todd wasn't anywhere around.

Pete McIntyre was still working in the yard. He gave me a quizzical look as I stretched out on the chaise lounge, facing the direction of the sun. "It's okay," I told him. "I've got permission from the big boss. Marcie said I should go outside. She's watching TV and Derek's taking a nap."

Pete looked doubtful. "That doesn't sound like Marcie. Did she fall on her head or something?"

"Oh, she's not such a bad kid." I smeared Bain de Soleil on my face, arms and legs. What a gorgeous day it was. I inhaled the clean, unpolluted air of Cape Cod. Pete and I started talking and I soon felt nice and relaxed.

Too bad Pete has red hair, I thought with a touch of regret. But like Bobbie-Lou always said, guys with red hair just don't cut it.

Guys with dark hair *did*. Like Todd Crowley, for example. "Hey, Pete—do you happen to know the guy that lives next door?"

"Todd Crowley?" Pete gave me a funny look. "How did you know him?"

"I met him out in the front yard right when my mother was leaving. He started talking to me."

"Todd sure doesn't waste much time," was Pete's comment.

The mention of Todd's name made my heart beat faster. I shut my eyes, enjoying the warmth of the sun, and thought about Todd:

His teeth gleamed as he smiled down at Ellen. "I knew it was you the moment we met. You were standing by the lawn sprinkler and I just knew."

Ellen blushed. "My," she said, looking through her lashes, "you sure don't waste much time, do you?"

Todd laughed softly. "I know what I want," he said, his dark eyes caressing her, "and it's you, Ellen . . ."

"ELLEN! ELLEN! Come here, quick!" Marcie's shrill voice was calling me. *Oh rats! Every time I have a good fantasy, somebody always manages to ruin it,* I thought to myself.

I pulled myself up from the lounge. "It was nice while it lasted," I told Pete. "I'd better go see what she's hollering about."

Marcie looked upset. "Do you know where Derek could be?" she asked. "I can't find him."

"What do you mean? Isn't he up in his room taking his nap?"

"He's not there." Her voice quivered. "I happened to walk by his room and I saw his bed was empty. But his nightgown was still there."

"Oh well," I said, "he probably woke up and went downstairs to—"

"Derek never goes *anywhere* without his nightgown," Marcie insisted. "I looked all over. Upstairs and down."

The two of us rushed up to Derek's room. He was nowhere around. His nightgown lay in a little ball on the floor next to his bed. "Look at this." Marcie held up the nightgown and pointed to a red stain. "Does that look like blood?"

"Don't be silly," I told her, but I was starting to feel a little nervous. We checked all the rooms upstairs, as well as the closets. The attic door was always kept locked, so Derek couldn't have gone there either. We knocked on Lisa's door, interrupting her phone conversation. I wondered if it was still the same call. No, she told us, she hadn't seen Derek.

We checked downstairs and the basement. We called out his name, but no Derek. "We've had a lot of mother's helpers, but nothing like this ever happened before," Marcie said ominously.

"Derek probably went outside to play. Or to visit a neighbor or something," I said, but Marcie kept shaking her head. "Derek *never* goes outside without me," she said stubbornly.

I ran back outside to the yard. Pete was getting ready to leave. He hadn't seen Derek either. "He's not out here," Pete said. "Derek doesn't go anywhere by himself." Pete asked me if there was any problem.

"No problem," I said hastily, and ran back into the house. *Where could Derek be?* Now I was getting worried. Marcie followed me while I checked the broom closet and under the sink. "Maybe Derek was kidnapped," she suggested. "They'll probably make my father pay a big ransom, I bet."

"Knock it off," I said, pulling up the sofa cushions. "Derek has to be around somewhere."

''Then again,'' she muttered darkly, ''maybe whoever took him doesn't want money. Maybe he was kidnapped by a sex prevert.''

''It's 'pervert,' not 'prevert'.'' Then I realized what she'd said. ''And knock it off, Marcie.''

''I bet my father will sue you for this,'' Marcie said. ''You're in big trouble. This is a negligence case. You were lying out in the yard sleeping and you should of been in the house watching him.''

''You *told* me to go outside,'' I protested. ''And furthermore, you were in the house and so was Lisa.''

''Uh-uh.'' Marcie shook her frizzy head vigorously. ''It's *your* responsibility. *You're* the mother's helper. You know what I keep wondering?'' she mused out loud. ''I wonder if that stain on the nightgown was blood or not.''

That was all it took to get me searching frantically again. The house was eerily quiet, except for the somber ticking of the big grandfather clock in the foyer. I was doing my second check of the coat closet when suddenly Lisa's voice—usually like a whisper—called out urgently from upstairs.

''MARCIE! ELLEN! COME UP HERE—QUICK!''

''What is it?'' Marcie yelled back.

''Is it Derek?'' I heard myself asking in a shaky voice.

Lisa shouted down to us even louder. ''Just come up here—*now*!''

An icy wave of fear washed over me.

Had Lisa found Derek?''

Had something happened to him?

4

''What *is* it?'' I gasped, stumbling to the top of the stairs. ''What's the matter?'' My heart was pounding in my throat. Horrible thoughts flashed through my mind:

> MOTHER'S HELPER CHARGED
> IN CHILD'S DISAPPEARANCE
> Chatam, MA—Ellen J. Gardner, fifteen, of Pawtucket, Rhode Island, was charged today with willful neglect in the mysterious disappearance of Derek Winner, age five, last seen taking a nap in his bedroom. ''She should've been watching him instead of laying outside getting a suntan,'' said the boy's sister, Marcella, ten who accused the mother's helper of . . .

Behind me, Marcie was panting up the stairs. ''What are you yelling about?'' she asked her sister.

Lisa stood at the top of the stairs, her arms folded. ''I want the truth,'' she said, looking at me.

''The truth about what?'' I croaked. Again, my imagination tormented me:

> *''What do you regret most about this dreadful incident?'' the reporter asked.*
> *''I bitterly regret that I never got to know more*

about that gorgeous guy next door," sobbed Ellen J. Gardner, as she was led away . . .

"You'll see," Lisa answered, turning around and heading into her room. I limped after her. My foot still hurt where I had twisted it.

What *would* we see in Lisa's bedroom? Derek? Had he smothered under a pile of shopping bags? Had he been poisoned drinking her instant hot-oil conditioning treatment? My heart thudded against my chest.

"Tell me the truth," Lisa said, deadly serious. "Which goes better with these slacks—the mauve sweater or this pink blouse?"

I collapsed on the bed, shaking.

"Well," Lisa demanded, "which one? The honest truth." She had pulled the pink blouse off its hanger and was posing with it. It was draped over her like the outfit on a paper doll.

"I thought you'd found Derek," I managed to choke.

Just as I said those words, the doorbell chimes rang, and a man's voice called out loudly, "Hey—anybody home?"

"That's probably the police," Marcie said. "I bet they found Derek's body someplace—all cut up in little pieces."

Twisted ankle and all, I bolted downstairs and unlatched the screen door.

I nearly fainted. It wasn't Derek, and it wasn't the police. It was Todd Crowley, looking absolutely gorgeous in a red T-shirt and white pants.

"Well, hello again," he smiled. "How's the new mother's helper doing?"

From behind me, Marcie's loud voice piped up,

''Oh—it's *you*. What do *you* want?''

''That's what I like about you, Marcie—you always make people feel so welcome,'' Todd said. ''I came over to borrow some ice. My mother asked if—'' He stopped talking and looked at me closely. ''Say—what's the matter? Is something wrong?''

''It's Derek.'' My words tripped over each other. ''I—we—can't find him. He was taking a nap in his room and—we don't know where he is.''

Marcie had opened the freezer and was dumping ice cubes into the ice bucket Todd had brought over. ''Here,'' she grumbled. ''How come you're always coming over for ice cubes anyhow? If your father is so rich, how come you can't afford a refrigerator that makes ice cubes, huh?''

''Our ice cube maker is on the blink,'' Todd informed her. ''And what's all this about Derek?''

''None of your business,'' Marcie muttered, but I chimed right in, saying, ''We looked everywhere and we can't find him.''

''Everywhere?'' Todd smiled again and gave me a wink. ''Don't worry—we'll find him.''

''And it had to happen on my first day,'' I kept on babbling.

''Hey, sweet stuff,'' Todd said, putting his arm around me, ''we'll find him. Let's take another look around.'' I was trembling, but I wasn't sure if it was because of Derek or because of Todd had put his arm around me.

''This isn't *your* house, Toad Crawly,'' Marcie yelled but Todd ignored her as he led me out of the kitchen. ''I have a theory,'' he said. ''I believe we're about to solve the Mystery of Disappearing Derek.'' We stood in the doorway of the laundry room. ''Look over there,'' Todd pointed.

"Where?" All I could see was a big pile of sheets and towels waiting to be washed.

But wait—the red and white striped beach towel seemed to be moving slightly. Then I heard a muffled sound—like somebody sucking a thumb.

Todd walked over and yanked the towel away. There—sitting on the floor all pink and smiling, his hair in damp ringlets—was little Derek.

I whirled around to confront Marcie.

"April fool!" she sang out as she ran from the laundry room, giggling. Derek jumped up and ran after her.

Todd stood there with his lopsided smile, shaking his head. "That kid never gives up, does she? She pulled the same stunt last summer with this blond girl named Ingrid. The girl quit on the spot. Too bad," he added, "that Ingrid was something wild. What an incredible body . . ."

I was astounded that Marcie could be so cruel. "Thank you, Todd," I said, swallowing hard. I couldn't think of anything else to say.

"I hope *you* won't do that—quit, I mean."

"Heck, no," I said fervently. If Marcie Winner thought I'd go running back to Pawtucket, she had another thought coming. Especially now that I'd met Todd Crowley!

Todd was leaning up against the kitchen sink, watching as I emptied fresh ice cubes into the teakwood bucket. "You know," he said softly, "our housekeeper saw you this morning when you drove up with your mother. She happened to be looking out of the window."

"She did? What did she say about me?" I asked breathlessly. It reminded me of a scene from a romance novel:

The housekeeper lifted the heavy curtains and peered out. "Master Todd," she whispered, "I have just seen the new mother's helper next door."

"Ah," he cried, "and what is she like?"

"She has a proud and noble bearing," the housekeeper told him. "She is shy, yet spirited . . . she—"

"She said, 'Here comes another sucker. I give this one a week at the most,' " Todd answered. It wasn't exactly what I was hoping to hear. Todd was studying me carefully. "Say—how old are you, anyhow?"

"Why? How old are *you*?"

"I'll be eighteen in October. I'm a Scorpio." His brown velvet eyes caught mine. "Scorpio is the sexiest male sign in the Zodiac."

I don't know what made me tell a lie, but I said, "I'm seventeen."

"Yeah? You don't look it—you look younger." A slow, easy smile spread over Todd's face. "Seventeen, huh? That's good—very good. You know what I think?"

But I never did find out what Todd was thinking because just then the doorbell rang. I heard Marcie open the front door and mumble something to whoever was there. The visitor mumbled something back. A few seconds later, a tall blond girl strode into the kitchen.

"I didn't know *you* were here, Todd," she drawled, throwing her arms around him and kissing his cheek. "Oh, I see Mumsy is getting ready for Happy Hour, hmmmm?"

I recognized that snippy boarding school accent

immediately. It was the snotty girl who had called Lisa earlier.

"Hey, Brandy baby—you're looking quite fine," Todd said, giving her a playful squeeze.

Well, that cleared up one thing—the name of the girl who had called Lisa. Brandy looked exactly the way she had sounded on the telephone—rich and thin and mean. She had a rich girl's hairstyle—dark blond hair with sun-bleached streaks, cut in one length around the chin so it looks good when you toss your hair. She had a dark, leathery tan, probably from being on Daddy's boat every summer, and muscular legs from playing field hockey at the exlusive boarding school she probably attended. Brandy dressed like a preppie—baggy white cotton shorts, a denim shirt and a heavy cotton sweater. Even on hot days, rich girls can wear those sweaters, because they don't seem to sweat like other people. Brandy wasn't pretty, but then again, she didn't have to be. She had an absolute self-confidence you're probably born with when your family has had a lot of money for a long time.

She looked at me coldly and said in an imperious voice, "You didn't give my message to Lisa."

"Well, the thing is . . ." Brandy made me positively tongue-tied.

"I hope you'll learn to write down a simple message," she said, her voice dripping sarcasm. "And maybe you'll even figure out how to read the telephone number."

I just couldn't help it. Brandy was so completely obnoxious, she made me defensive. I started talking in a high, squeaky voice, imitating the little black maid in *Gone With the Wind*.

"Lordy, lordy, Miz Brandy," I squeaked out, rolling my eyes to the ceiling, "I don't know *nothin'* 'bout writin' messages!"

Todd started to laugh. So did Marcie, who had sneaked into the kitchen to hear what was going on.

Brandy's pale blue eyes narrowed as they slid over me. "Toddy-poo, you'd better not keep the mother's helper from her chores. After all, she *is* a working girl. And besides, Mumsy *needs* her ice," she said, giving Todd a little push as he opened the back door. "Maybe we'll see you at B.J.'s party," she called out.

With that, she shot me a triumphant smirk and turned on her heel, bumping into Marcie, who let out a yelp. "You stepped on my toe!" Marcie cried out.

"Serves you right, bratkins," Brandy retorted. "Is Lisa upstairs in her room?"

"Go see for yourself, creepo. I'm not your servant." Marcie stuck her tongue out at Brandy, who was running up to Lisa's room.

Grabbing a can of grape soda from the refrigerator, Marcie said, "Ugh—I hate that Brandy Simms. I don't know how my dumb sister can stand her."

For a fleeting moment, I felt a sense of kinship with Marcie. Although I'd been furious with her for the nasty trick she'd pulled, I was ten times angrier at Brandy Simms. Sure, Marcie was a brat, but anyone who hated Brandy Simms couldn't be all that bad. I recalled a proverb I had read: "The enemy of my enemy is my friend."

Marcie left the kitchen, and I sat down exhausted at the table to think about everything that had happened.

It occurred to me that I had experienced almost every human emotion there was—anticipation and letdown . . . excitement and boredom . . .jealousy and envy . . . fear and joy . . . love and hate.

And all in the space of about two and a half hours!

5

Monday nite, June 24

Dear Bobbie-Lou,

Greetings, from Cape Cod.

First the Good News—Mom & I found the house without any trouble.

Now the Bad News—maybe we should have kept on driving!

Remember how you thought this job sounded like the plot in *Love by the Sea*? Wrong, wrong, wrong.

Marcella (alias Marcie) is beyond believing. All I can say is if they had a Brat Olympics, Marcie would get the Gold Medal.

Derek is cute & sweet, but I don't think he is on full wattage, poor thing.

AND THE VERY WORST PART OF IT ALL IS THAT THEY HATE THE BEACH!!!!! MARCIE SAYS THEY *NEVER* GO SWIMMING!! No wonder they had a zillion mother's helpers before me. I should have known this job was too good to be true.

They also have a sister, Lisa—she's 16 & looks like a movie star. She has beautiful clothes. I get to iron them all.

There is one bright spot—I met the most gorgeous hunk. His name is Todd Crowley & he lives next door. Will keep you posted on my romance (if it ever develops!!).

Have a good trip down South, y'all & write soon.

Love,
Ellen,
(alias Cinderella)

Monday night, June 24

Dear Mom,

I just wanted to drop you a quick note before I go to bed to tell you everything's fine here.

Marcella and Derek are very nice and very smart like you figured they'd be. We are getting along great.

Met Mrs. W at dinner—she sends you her regards. Mr. W is out of town on business—he'll be back Wednesday.

Good luck on your exam. I know you'll do great.

Love,
Ellen,
(alias Your Daughter, The Writer-to-Be)

P.S. I promise you I will not lie around the beach all summer.

6

Tuesday morning brought heavy, dark skies and pouring rain.

Oh, rats, I thought, listening to the downpour as it slapped against my window. I had planned to sit out in the backyard and maybe catch a glimpse of Todd Crowley. No such luck today.

"It's like a flood out there," Grandma Brill fretted at breakfast. "Such a gloomy day."

Then the thought hit me: *What in the world was I going to do all day long with Marcie and Derek?*

Evidently Mrs. Winner had been wondering about that, too.

"Ellen, dear," she greeted me as I slid into my seat at the kitchen table, "you mustn't let the children just sit around and watch TV all day. You need to get them involved in creative activities."

I had met Mrs. Winner the night before, but only for a few minutes. As soon as she got home from the office, she had to rush out again for a meeting with an elderly client. I was kind of surprised when I met her. For someone who's supposed to be such a hotshot lawyer, she has this awful, old-fashioned hairdo that's sprayed and teased into a huge flip on both sides of her head. It makes her look like the Queen of Hearts on a playing card.

Before I could even say "Good morning", she handed me a business envelope with my name on it. Inside, typed on red-lined legal paper, it read:

SUGGESTED ACTIVITIES W/CHILDREN

1. Exercises and/or calisthenics
2. Sewing and/or needlework
3. Educational games/puzzles.
4. Go over arithmetic exercises (NOTE: Marcella has had problems with arithmetic this year)
5. Creative activities (i.e., reading, painting*)

*NOTE: The paint-by-numbers sets are in the basement. Please make sure to paint there! Do *not* paint upstairs!

''I thought the list would be helpful. Don't you?'' Mrs. Winner asked.

''Oh, er, very helpful,'' I said. I could just see Marcie curling up with a nice book on arithmetic. Not to mention doing calisthenics.

Mrs. Winner gathered up her papers from the kitchen table. ''And Ellen dear, don't forget the laundry. It's been piling up, I'm afraid.'' She got her raincoat and umbrella from the hall closet and popped her head back into the kitchen once more. ''And whenever you have a spare moment, you can always run the iron over the clothes in the laundry basket.''

I reread the list of activities while I ate my Raisin Bran. *Dream on, Mrs. Winner*, I thought, smiling to myself.

When Marcie came down for breakfast, I showed her the list. She ripped it up. ''Sometimes,'' said

Marcie, "I don't think my mother even has a clue."

I quickly discovered that Marcie's most creative activity was figuring out what snack to have. The rain made her hungrier than usual, and all morning she was in and out of the kitchen—opening and closing the refrigerator, or asking me to toast something.

"I'm going to get the laundry and ironing out of the way," I told Marcie who was flicking the TV channel selector in the den. Derek sat on the floor playing with his toys. I put in a load of towels and filled the steam iron.

As I started to tackle the pile of clothes in the laundry basket, the back doorbell and the buzzer on the clothes drier both sounded. I emptied the drier and ran to answer the door.

It was Pete McIntyre, rain dripping off his yellow slicker. I remembered Grandma Brill saying that Pete might come by in the morning to do some work in the house.

"Might as well do it today," he said cheerfully, wiping his sneakers on the rubber mat. "It's no day to be outdoors."

I was glad to see Pete. At least he was someone to talk to. Marcie and Derek were glued to the TV set, Grandma Brill was upstairs writing letters, and Lisa had slept over Brandy's—or was it Mandy's—house.

"I'll keep you company," Pete said, putting his toolbox down on the laundry room floor. "Mrs. Winner wanted some shelves put up here."

He glanced around at the freshly ironed clothes hanging everywhere—on the drying rack, the doorknob, the top of the washing machine.

"Wow," he said, shaking his head. "You could

make a whole career out of doing Lisa's ironing.''

It was the first time I'd gotten a good look at Pete without his sunglasses. Except for his freckles, he was kind of cute. His eyes were the colour of blueberries and he had a nice smile.

But that red hair! What a pity to waste those nice blue eyes on a guy with red hair.

''So,'' he asked, ''how's it going?''

''Are you kidding? I'm about as popular as acne,'' I said, launching into the story of Derek's disappearance and how Todd Crowley had come to my rescue.

''Old Toddy is a regular knight in shining armor,'' Pete said as he measured the walls for the shelves, making pencil marks in various spots.

I kept pumping Pete for information about Todd, but he only gave me grudging details. I learned that Todd went to a private shcool, that he drove a bright red Camaro that was his pride and joy, and that his father was a rich businessman who had moved to the Cape five years ago.

It was very comfortable talking and working with Pete. I never knew a boy who was so easy to talk to.

''Mrs. Winner wants everything done around the house before Mr. W comes back,'' Pete said.

''What's Mr. Winner like?'' I asked, setting down the iron. ''Everybody seems kind of afraid of him.''

''What is Mr. Winner like?'' Pete thought about that for a moment. ''You wouldn't believe me if I told you.''

I was just about to ask him what he meant when in marched Marcie and Derek.

''You're the most boring mother's helper we've ever had,'' Marcie complained. ''You're supposed to keep us entertained, but all you do is laundry and ironing."

"Ellen's always goofing off," Pete winked.

Happy to shut off the iron, I turned to Marcie and said, "Fine with me. What do you feel like doing? We could play Monopoly." Marcie shook her head.

"Scrabble? Careers?"

"Baby games," Marcie sulked.

"Hey, Marcie—did you ever play Treasure Hunt? It's a lot of fun. My mother used to play it with me."

"Your *mother*? She played *games* with you?" Marcie looked astonished.

"Sure. She taught me a lot of games." I explained Treasure Hunt to Marcie. "What I do is think up clues and you have to figure them out. One clue leads to another and finally to the treasure."

Marcie looked interested. "I'm good at things like that," she bragged. "I watch quiz shows all the time."

I gathered up Lisa's clothes to bring upstairs. "You have to give me at least ten minutes to hide the clues in my room," I told Marcie. I felt virtuous as I trudged up the stairs. This certainly fell into the category of "educational games" on Mrs. Winner's list of Suggested Activities.

In my room, I shut the door and looked around for good hiding places. I was sitting at Marcie's desk writing clues when I heard pounding on the door.

"Give me a break, you guys," I called out. "It isn't even five minutes yet."

"Hurry up," Marcie shouted back. "Me and Derek are sick of waiting."

I finished writing and hid the clues carefully. When I opened the door Marcie and Derek practically tumbled inside. Pete stood in back of them, grinning. "I thought I'd sit in on this," he said.

"Marcie invited me."

"Pete can't play," Marcie explained. "He's just gonna watch."

I sat down on the little rocking chair and handed Marcie clue Number One, which said: "A STEREO CAN MAKE A RACKET."

She paced back and forth like a little tiger, looking all around. "This is dumb. There's no stereo in here. You're cheating."

But Derek tugged at Marcie's arm and pointed to where my tennis racket stood on the floor. "Good boy," Marcie cried. She lifted it and under the handle found a tiny piece of folded white paper.

"See that?" she chortled. "I told you I was good at stuff like this."

The second clue read: "IN WINTER, I GO SKATING ON FROZEN PONDS." Marcie figured that one right away, as soon as she spotted the jar of Pond's cold cream on the dresser.

Clue Number Three was a snap: "PRINCE CHARMING FOUND CINDERELLA'S SLIPPER." Marcie ran over and pulled out my terry-cloth slipper from under the bed as Pete cheered her on.

The final clue said: "NOW IS THE TIME FOR ALL GOOD MEN TO COME TO THE AID OF ELLEN GARDNER." It was hidden under my clock radio and it only took Marcie a few seconds to figure it out. She pulled out a slip of paper on which I'd written: "CONGRATULATIONS—YOU ARE A GENIUS. YOU FOUND THE TREASURE."

Marcie jumped up and down while Derek giggled and jumped along with her. "I found the treasure, I found the treasure," she cried.

The commotion brought Grandma Brill rushing

out of her room, still holding the letter she had been writing. "What is it? What's wrong?" she asked frantically.

"Everything's fine," Pete reassured her. "Marcie guessed all the clues and now she's going to get the treasure."

"Is there really a treasure?" Marcie asked, her pale cheeks pink with excitement.

"You bet," said Pete. "It's lunch from Captain Chicken. My treat."

"Ooohhh," Marcie squealed. "I *love* Captain Chicken."

"Well, figure out what you and Derek want. Ellen's going to come along with me and help carry the food." He gave me a quick wink.

"No fair," Marcie protested. She had noticed the wink. "I want to come, too." Luckily Pete and Grandma Brill insisted she would catch a cold if she went out in the rain.

I didn't care if I got soaked. I was happy to get out of the house, even for a few minutes. Grandma Brill gave me a rainslicker from the hall closet and an umbrella. Marcie decided she and Derek would have the Henny Penny Surprise.

"My truck is parked out in front," Pete said.

When I saw his truck, I cracked up. It was bright green with a drawing of a masked man mowing the lawn and a sign that read: "THE LAWN RANGER. YARD WORK AND VERY ODD JOBS."

Then, as I stopped laughing, I noticed a strange pattern on the ground. What a sickening sight.

It had been raining so hard all morning that everywhere I looked, there were washed-up worms!

Long pink ones that looked like tree branches.

Small gray worms. Dead worms. Wriggling worms.

"Oh, disgusting," I yelled. "It's like Worm World out here."

I have this phobia about worms that dates back to my childhood. I was helping my dad plant some vegetables and as I started to dig, I dug right into a worm! Half a worm, actually. It was still wriggling even though it was cut in half. It made me sick. Even now, just the sight of a worm makes me gag.

"I'd die if a worm ever touched me," I shuddered as I told Pete about my worm phobia. He was pretty understanding about it. He said I didn't have to get out of the truck when we went to Captain Chicken.

"This is great," I said. "I feel like a prisoner who gets to go to the prison yard for fifteen minutes."

"I can tell you're happy in your job," Pete said. He stopped at a takeout restaurant that had a huge sign of a chicken wearing a sea captain's hat. There weren't many cars in the parking lot, probably because of the bad weather, so it didn't take Pete long to get the food. Before I knew it, he came back outside with two big yellow bags decorated with Captain Chicken.

"This is the best fried chicken you ever tasted," Pete said. "I figured you could use a break from opening sardine cans."

"You got that right," I said, wishing he would drive slower so we could stay out longer.

As we walked up the Winners' driveway, I had to dodge so many worms I nearly dropped the bags of food. "This is worse than Worm World," I whimpered. "It's Worm Galaxy. They don't have this many worms in all of Rhode Island."

Marcie was waiting by the back door, her face pressed against the screen. "What took you so long?" she demanded. "We're starving."

"Well, it's like this," Pete said as he put the food on the kitchen counter. "Ellen had to walk real slow and carefully on account of the worms."

As I set the table and put the food out on plates, I listened to Pete telling Marcie about my worm phobia.

"What a wimp she is," Marcie snickered. "Worms can't hurt you."

"Please," I said, "don't even *talk* about those disgusting creatures." We sat down to eat. Pete was right—this really was the best fried chicken I had ever tasted. I was reaching for my second piece when suddenly Pete yelled out, "Watch it, Ellen—there's a worm on your plate!"

I jumped up and let out a shriek as Pete snatched a long, thin French fry from my plate and waved it in front of me.

"Don't scare me like that," I said. "You'll give me a heart attack."

Marcie put down her chicken leg and gave me a funny look. "Scared of little bitty worms," she said to nobody in particular.

There was a strange smile on her face.

7

It was still pouring rain on Wednesday morning.

I felt so tired I couldn't get out of bed. It seemed as if I had been dreaming about Todd the whole night long. He kept driving by in his red Camaro, but every time I went over to the car, he would drive away. No wonder I was so exhausted.

As the rain pounded against the window, I lay there feeling depressed. Another long day of not seeing Todd. Another long day of keeping Marcie and Derek entertained. By now, I was burned out on Treasure Hunt, sick to death of Let's Pretend, and ready to barf if I played one more game of Monopoly.

I was racking my brain for ideas about what to do when I heard voices in the kitchen. Marcie and Grandma Brill were arguing.

Marcie? Up before *me?*

Uh-oh. I glanced at my clock radio and nearly flipped. It was after ten o'clock! I never sleep that late. Then I heard Mrs. Winner's voice and I knew I'd better get downstairs as fast as I could.

Which is why I didn't even bother to brush my teeth or comb my hair. I just threw on my bathrobe, ran down to the kitchen as fast as I could, and slid into my seat.

And guess who was sitting at the kitchen table, big as life, eating a blueberry muffin.

''Well, hello there, sleepyhead,'' Todd Crowley greeted me. ''Did you have pleasant dreams?''

I felt totally mortified. Bad enough I looked like something out of a horror show. But even worse, I couldn't open my mouth to talk. I hadn't brushed my teeth, and my mouth tasted like I had just gargled with fertilizer.

''You've got to try these,'' Todd said, handing me a big plate with the most scrumptious-looking muffins, chock-full of blueberries. ''Our housekeeper made them this morning. My mother told me to bring them over here because Mrs. Winner loves Edna's muffins.''

''Oh, sure. Righto.'' Marcie made a rude noise. ''Like everyone really believes your mother actually woke up before two in the afternoon. You're just trying to score Brownie points, that's all.''

''Now, now, Marcella,'' Mrs. Winner said absently.

''Well, it's true and you *know* it.'' Marcie polished off yet another muffin and then turned her full attention to me.

''It's about time *you* showed up,'' she said, pointing to the clock. ''We figured you were dead—but no such luck.''

''Not acceptable, Marcella,'' Mrs. Winner said. She had been looking over some papers, her glasses perched at the end of her nose. She put everything down and gave me a tight little smile. ''Well, Ellen, I didn't realize you were such a late riser. I need to go over a few things with you before I leave for the office.''

Grandma Brill was busy clattering around, rinsing off the breakfast dishes and scouring the frying pan. Nobody can make as much noise with dishes as poor Grandma.

''Oh, do be quiet, Mother,'' Mrs. Winner said irritably. ''Stop making all that noise until I finish chatting with Ellen.

''Just some little things that need to be done around the house,'' she said, handing me another typed list. ''Mr. Winner will be flying back this evening, and we want everything in the house to look just so, don't we?''

She went on to explain that their cleaning woman was away and wouldn't be in until Monday. And so, of course, everyone had to do their part.

As she spoke, I had been trying to slink down in my chair to hide myself from Todd. That's why I didn't even notice Lisa, making her grand entrance. It took me a few seconds to realize why the conversation had stopped.

It simply wasn't fair. Even with her hair hanging wet from the shower . . . even without a drop of makeup, Lisa Winner looked absolutely beautiful. As if that wasn't bad enough, she was wearing a gorgeous, peach-coloured silky robe.

Naturally, she sat down next to me. I felt like a Teenage Bag Lady.

Todd couldn't pull his eyes off her. ''Wow,'' he breathed, ''I didn't know anybody could look *that* good first thing in the morning!''

Grandma Brill stopped rinsing and clattering. She rushed over to the table and passed the plate of muffins to Lisa. ''Todd brought these over. He knows you like Edna's muffins.''

''No thank you,'' Lisa said in her baby voice. ''I'm on a diet. Just juice, Grandma.''

Grandma Brill scampered over to the refrigerator, took out some oranges and put them in the juicer. Then she brought Lisa a tall glass of freshly squeezed orange juice.

"Hey!" Marcie yelled. "How come you never squeeze orange juice for *me*?"

"You don't even *like* orange juice," Grandma protested. "You take one sip and you never finish it."

"That's not the point," Marcie insisted. "I can't *stand* the way everybody always jumps up and waits on Lisa. Why can't she squeeze her own orange juice for a change? There's nothing wrong with *her* legs!"

"*I'll* say," Todd leered. "Nothing wrong at all."

"Now, now, sweetie," Mrs. Winner said. She was making notes on her pocket calendar, hardly paying attention.

Marcie slammed her cereal bowl on the table. "See that—you're not even listening to me," she said. "How come you never listen to me?"

Mrs. Winner was staring out the kitchen window. "The rain seems to be letting up a bit," she said. "I think I'll head into the office now." She gathered up her beige raincoat, beige umbrella and a beige canvas bag that had been sitting on the empty chair next to her.

"Now you be a good little angelkins, Derek," she said, ruffling his curls. She blew a kiss to Lisa, then another in Marcie's direction. "Oh, Marcella, sweetums, do keep yourself busy today so you won't snack so much."

There was a silence. Marcie just sat there. Her face was all puffed up in anger, but she didn't say one word. I actually felt sorry for her.

But I felt even sorrier for myself. All the while, I had been sneaking peeks at Todd. He hardly took his eyes off Lisa from the moment she glided into the kitchen. You would have to be deaf, dumb, and blind not to know Todd was hung up on Lisa Winner. But she didn't seem interested in him at all. She just sat there, twirling a strand of silky brown hair and sipping her orange juice with a dreamy little smile on her face.

It made me want to gag. Why was life so unfair? Couldn't Todd see past Lisa's beautiful face? Why, why, why? It was the Eternal Mystery of Life that Bobbie-Lou and I had often pondered: Why are guys so *dumb*?

I felt myself drifting off, summoning a fantasy to comfort myself:

> *Suddenly Todd turned around, staring at Ellen in wonder. "How blind I have been," he said. "All this time, I thought I was in love with Lisa, but I was really in love with you. So what if Lisa Winner is beautiful and rich and popular and has gorgeous clothes and looks good without makeup . . . that's not everything. You, Ellen," he smiled tenderly, "you have character . . ."*

"Ellen. Earth to Ellen. Hey, wake up!" Todd's voice jarred me out of my daydream. "Wake up, Ellen, you look like you're in another world."

I sat up, embarrassed, and concentrated on finishing my Raisin Bran. Lisa twirled her hair some more, while Todd watched, as fascinated as a cobra under the spell of a snake charmer. As soon as Lisa excused herself, Todd stood up abruptly and said he had better get back home. After everyone left, I cleaned up the kitchen and then changed into my oldest jeans for the Big Cleanup.

For the next few hours, all of us worked like busy little bees. Even Lisa pitched in, sort of. It took her a while to comb her closet for the right outfit, "something old and tacky". Well, I wish I owned something as tacky as the outfit she finally decided to wear—a light blue denim jumpsuit with a wide red belt that made her waistline look about six inches wide. Then she tied a silk scarf around her hair.

Lisa's contribution to the clean-up campaign was an attempt to straighten out her bedroom. What she actually did, though, was to take all the clothes she had lying around on the floor and the beds and put them into the clothes hamper to be washed.

Derek decided he wanted to help me. He loved to polish things, so I let him shine the faucets and the mirror in the downstairs bathroom. Then he followed me to the family room and I let him spray pledge on the furniture. We were almost through dusting the bookcase when Derek stopped and pointed to a book on the top shelf.

"Boo," he said. "My boo."

"Not *boo*, Derek. It's *book*," I corrected him. I took it down from the shelf and saw it was a beautifully illustrated volume of *Best Loved Mother Goose Rhymes*. It looked as if it had never even been opened. I gave it to Derek, who beamed as he reverently turned the pages.

"El," he said, pointing to the book. "El do boo."

I was getting quite good at translating Derek's words. "Are you saying you want me to read this book to you, Derek?" I asked, and he nodded. "Well, all right—just let me finish up in here and then we'll take a reading break."

I zipped through the dusting, and then Derek started getting restless, so the two of us plopped down on the tweed carpet in the family room. "What a beautiful book this is," I said. "I didn't know you liked books, Derek." There was an inscription on the inside cover that said, "To sweet little Derek. Merry Christmas from Julienne and Ty."

As I read, Derek became really excited. He smiled and pointed to all the illustrations, saying "More, more, El." I realized then that Derek was a lot smarter than anyone gave him credit for. Maybe he didn't say much, but he was certainly aware of everything going on.

I decided to play little games with the book. "Okay, Derek," I said, "show me *Humpty-Dumpty*. Show me *The Cat and the Fiddle*."

The two of us were so engrossed in the book that we jumped when a loud voice behind us cried accusingly, "What are you doing?" It was Marcie, slurping on a grape Popsicle. She grabbed the book out of my hand. "Oh, so that's where it is. I wondered what happened to that book. Julienne gave it to Derek last Christmas."

"Derek loves having somebody read to him," I said. "Do you ever read to him, Marcie?"

"Huh," she snorted. "I hate to read."

"Are you serious?" I asked, amazed. It's hard to believe some people actually don't like reading. Mom and I both love books. But now that I thought about it, I had never noticed many books or magazines around the house, except for big volumes of law journals and reference books. There were hardly any children's books around, not even in Derek's and Marcie's rooms.

Grandma Brill, as far as I could see, was the only reader in the house, and hers were mainly romance novels and women's magazines from the local library.

Marcie gave a shrug. "My mother and father don't have time to read to us," she explained, as if to defend them. "And Grandma always loses her place. And besides, she's always cooking."

"My mother says if you like to read, you'll never be lonely," I told them.

Marcie considered that for a moment. "Well, even if I did like to read," she said, "I wouldn't know *what* to read."

For the next few minutes, I launched into a discussion of the books I had loved when I was a kid. "My favorite was *Anne of Green Gables*. And *Little Women*." I smiled, remembering. "Oh, and *Heidi*. I loved *Heidi*."

"I knew a girl named Heidi Hancock," Marcie offered. "She was in my class last year. I hated her."

"You know," I said, "until I read *Heidi*, I would never eat cheese. But in the book, Heidi and her grandfather were always eating bread and cheese up in the mountains where they lived. It sounded so delicious I decided I wanted cheese, too. I used to pretend I was Heidi whenever I had a cheese sandwich."

I should have known not to bring up the subject of food. "Hey," Marcie complained, "it's way past lunchtime. No wonder I'm hungry. I want a sardine sandwich."

If I have to fiddle around with the key in the sardine can one more time, I thought to myself, *I'll flip*. "Hey, listen, Marcie," I said, "let's me and you and Derek play *Heidi*. We'll have bread and cheese like they did, okay?"

"Yeah," Marcie said excitedly. "I can be Heidi and Derek can be the grandfather."

"What about me? Who should I be?"

"You," she decided, "can be the mother's helper."

"But Heidi didn't have a mother. That's why she

had to go live with her grandfather in the Alps."

"Okay then," Marcie said after a moment, "you can be the ugly witch." She pulled Derek up from the floor. "Come on, little brother. Let's make believe we live up on a great big mountain and we're going to have lunch."

I followed them into the kitchen and started to fix three cheese sandwiches.

"Not that way," Marcie ordered. "I want a grilled-cheese sandwich."

I wasn't in the mood to stand and fuss. I still had other chores to do, including ironing. "Listen," I told her, "do you think Heidi had grilled cheese way up on a mountaintop? No. They had a hunk of dry bread and goat cheese."

"Yuck," Marcie said with a grimace. "It's too dry that way."

"Then forget about playing," I told her. "Tomorrow I figured we could play *Anne of Green Gables*, and you could be Anne. But not if you're going to give me a hard time. Forget it."

"Don't get so huffy," Marcie said. "I'll eat that yucky sandwich. But you better give me a real big glass of grape soda."

"One big grape coming up," I sang out, opening the refrigerator. I felt a tiny sense of victory.

Her mouth full of cheese and white bread, Marcie announced, "Tomorrow I'll be Anne of Green Gables and Derek can be my brother. What did Anne have for lunch?"

"Peanut butter," I told her with a perfectly straight face. "Anne of Green Gables hated sardines."

Dinner that night was going to be late, Grandma Brill informed us, because Mr. Winner's flight was delayed by bad weather. She was scampering around the kitchen, cooking up a storm.

Strangely enough, Marcie didn't even complain about dinner being late. She was suddenly on her best behavior. She even went upstairs and put on a dress when her mother called from the office to tell everyone to look nice. Derek's mop of curls was combed down, and he even agreed not to carry his nightgown around. Grandma Brill changed out of her Reeboks into a pair of white sandals. And even Mrs. Winner put on a light blue dress when she came home from the office. It was the first time I had ever seen her wear anything except beige. She looked nice.

Lisa, of course, didn't have to be coaxed. She tried on three or four outfits and then decided to wear a yellow jumpsuit. She had gone out that very afternoon to buy it. "I'm doing it for Father," she explained very seriously. "So I'll look nice."

Then and there I should have realized Martin Winner was something out of the ordinary. I mean, nobody I know calls their father "Father". It was "Dad" or "Daddy" or "Pops". Even "Pa".

But "Father"? That only happened on television and in books.

Marcie and Derek were peeking out of the window, watching for Mr. Winner. "There's Father now," Marcie cried excitedly. "I see his cab outside." Everyone rushed over to the front door.

I felt out of place. This was a family thing, so I decided to give them some privacy for a few minutes. I went upstairs and changed into a skirt instead of my white pants. Then I went back downstairs.

When I walked into the kitchen, Mr. Winner had his back to me and was listening to Mrs. Winner tell a long, involved story about an insurance adjuster. I just stood there quietly, waiting to be introduced.

There didn't seem to be anything unusual about Martin Winner. He was thin, not very tall and he was wearing a light gray suit. I couldn't imagine what all the fuss was about.

Then he turned around.

When I looked him full in the face, I thought my throat would close up.

I felt like I recognized Martin Winner. It was as if I'd known him for a long time, since I was a little kid and Mrs. Eberly next door used to give me Bible story coloring books.

I remember there was always this certain Crayola crayon—a light brown—that I would use to color His hair and . . .

"You must be Ellen Gardner," Mr. Winner intoned solemnly. I was stunned. His voice was like no other I had ever heard. It sounded like it came from far, far away.

Martin Winner had light brown hair, the exact color of that Crayola. It was kind of longish and parted in the middle. He had sorrowful brown eyes.

I could picture him standing in a desert instead of near the dishwasher . . . I imagined him wearing a blue robe and sandals instead of a light gray suit . . . the way he held out his hands . . . and . . .

So that's what Pete meant! No wonder Martin Winner was such a successful lawyer. The way he looked, the way he spoke . . . he could win over any jury!

I swallowed and tried to answer him, but no words would come.

Marcie broke the silence. "See that? I told you Ellen is just as dumb as all the others."

8

Sunday nite, June 30

Dear Bobbie-Lou,

This job gets crazier & crazier. Finally got to meet Mr. W the other night. I'll tell you about him when I get home. It's so strange. I'm afraid if I write about him, a bolt of lightning will strike me down.

Anyhow—here's what happened on my First Weekend on Scenic Cape Cod. Big Sat. nite event was having to go food shopping for Mrs. W, accompanied by the Talented Team of Marcella & Derek—they chased each other around the market & acted so awful, the ass't manager yelled at me (he thought I was their sister—horrors).

Speaking of sisters, Lisa was supposed to pick us up in an hour at the market since Mr. & Mrs. W had to go out to dinner with a client & Grandma was playing bingo. But Lisa never came. We waited almost 2 hrs. & no Lisa. Marcie was yelling, Derek was crying, etc. I didn't have enough money left to take a cab back. Finally got the idea to call Pete, the yard boy. Luckily he was home. He came by & gave us a ride home.

Turned out Dippy Lisa completely forgot about us. She'd been so busy at her friend Brandy's beach club fixing everyone's hair that it slipped her mind. Knowing Lisa's mind, you could believe it.

As if that wasn't enough excitement for one weekend, today Mr. & Mrs. W decided to give me the Big Tour. We went for a Sunday ride but the traffic was so bad, we didn't get very far or see very much. I'm going to have to figure out some way to get to see the Cape on my own or during the week.

Well, it was a ride to remember—Marcie, Derek, Grandma B. and me were all squashed together in the back seat. Mrs. W didn't want the window open too much because she didn't want to mess her hair (a chain saw couldn't mess her hair it's so teased and sprayed) & the air conditioner was broken so you can imagine how comfortable everyone was & what a good mood Marcie was in.

The highlight of the day was stopping for ice cream at this place called Sweet Tooth. Marcie & Derek wanted sundaes—I did, too—but Mrs. W (the Big Spender) said real loud, "Ellen—I'm sure you're watching your weight. Wouldn't you rather just have a mini-cone?"

Can you believe it? I was mortified. Plus I was dying to have their specialty, the Chocolate Fantasy Sundae, but what could I say? Even as I'm writing this, I'm having a fantasy about that Chocolate Fantasy Sundae.

On the way back, Derek dropped his sundae all over the car seat. Grandma & Marcie argued all the way. Derek decided to sit on my lap and made me all hot and sticky. Mr. & Mrs. W talked nonstop about things in the office and didn't pay any attention to any of us.

I wonder if that's why Marcie and Derek act like they do. It's probably the only way they can get any attention from their parents. Mr. & Mrs. W are so wrapped up in their law firm, they don't even have time for their own kids.

Oh, well. What keeps me going is thinking about the money I'll make this summer and getting my E.T. (Electronic typewriter), writing a book, getting rich & famous, etc.

The other thing that keeps me going is seeing Todd Crowley. Alias Todd terrific. He stopped over an hour ago (I think it was to see if Lisa was home—she wasn't—did I tell you he likes her?). Rats. He is *so* gorgeous.

Write soon. I need moral support. I'm sending this letter to your Nawth Carolina address so you'll get it faster.

Your suffering writer friend,
E. Jane Gardner
(how does that sound for a pen name?)

Sunday eve, June 30

Dear Mom,

It was great talking to you this morning. That funny noise you heard was Marcie listening in on the extension phone in the den. She does wacky stuff like that & plays telephone tricks. She likes to kid around. Ha-ha!

Went for a ride this afternoon—Mr. & Mrs. W wanted to show me the Cape. We went all over—there's so much to see. It was great. Then we had sundaes at this fabulous place.

Do you realize tomorrow makes one whole week I've been here?

Love & XXX,
Ellen

P.S. When you come down to visit, I'll take you to this place called Sweet Tooth—I'll even treat you to a Chocolate Fantasy Sundae.

9

On Monday morning, Mr. Winner went into the office at the crack of dawn, and Grandma Brill went away with her group, the Merry Senior Citizens, on a boat trip to Martha's Vineyard. Mrs. Winner was alone in the kitchen when I came downstairs.

"Oh, Ellen, dear," she said, looking up at me, "I wanted to know if you had any plans for this coming Sunday?"

"Uh—not really," I said, wondering what she was leading up to.

She smiled brightly. "Well, then, how would you like the day off?"

"Oh," I said. "Fine." This was a pleasant surprise. I had been wondering about getting time off and I'd been trying to work up the courage to ask Mrs. Winner about it. I had been there for a week now and time off hadn't been mentioned. I felt like I was on 24-hour call.

"You see, Ellen, we're invited to a barbecue in Stoughton on Sunday—my husband's sister—they have a Cousins Club get-together every year."

"That's nice," I said politely.

"Yes—well, of course, it's a *family* thing," she said, with a tinkly little laugh. "I mean, if you *really* wanted to tag along, you could. But then, you really wouldn't *know* anybody there, would you? Seeing how it's a *family* get-together and . . ." Her voice trailed off.

What Mrs. Winner was saying so persuasively to me was that I'd be as welcome as a pimple on Prom Night.

"Oh, no—really," I responded, going along with her, "it's nice of you, but I'd just as soon hang around and maybe catch up on my reading and letter writing and all that."

"Well, if you don't mind." She sounded relieved.

Did I *mind*? I was overjoyed to be alone. Ecstatic, in fact, at the thought of a day without Marcie. No sardine cans to open, no games to think up, no insults to listen to.

"Don't mind *what*?" From out of nowhere, Marcie had materialized. She was still in red pajamas, and she must have slept in a weird position during the night, because her hair stuck up in one big chunk. She looked like she was in a bad mood.

And when she found out what we had been talking about, her mood got even worse.

"That's not *fair*!" she hollered. "How come Ellen can stay home but I have to go to that dumb barbecue?"

Mrs. Winner leaned over and said in her let's-be-reasonable voice, "Now, sweetums, Ellen isn't *family*. And besides, don't you want to see your cousins on Sunday?"

"I *hate* my cousins," Marcie yelled even louder. "Those mean little show-offs."

The two of them argued back and forth while I sat there planning what I would do on Sunday, glorious Sunday. I could lie in the sun for a couple of hours and maybe get to see Todd. I could read one of the romance novels Grandma Brill got from the library. I could fill up the tub and soak in it for a whole hour without someone yelling, "Come on out quick—I gotta go!"

The argument went on. "Me and Derek have to sit in the hot sun and listen to Creepy Courtney and Horrible Hillary brag about their dancing lessons," Marcie complained.

Mrs. Winner sighed patiently. "Now, Marcella, we go through this silly business every summer. It'll be fun to eat barbecue and play in Cousin Brenda's pool. You're such a good swimmer, too."

"Marcie knows how to *swim*?" I blurted out in surprise. I had thought she was afraid of the water.

"Of *course* I know how to swim," Marcie snorted. "I took swimming lessons at the Y since I was a little kid." She looked up at her mother and said, "Hey, Mom, remember when Julienne used to take me to the Y and I won first prize in the—"

"Of course, sweetkins," Mrs. Winner broke in with another sigh. "But what I can't understand is why you used to love the water and now you won't go near it. It doesn't make sense."

Suddenly, it all made sense to me.

It wasn't that Marcie hated the water but that she hated the way she looked in a bathing suit!

That sinking feeling was all too familiar to me. Until about two years ago, I'd been chubby, too. But then, when Mom went on Weight Watchers, we both started eating differently and I trimmed down. Even now, though, I can still remember how depressing it was to have to buy my clothes in the Pretty-Plus Department.

I also had a hunch that Cousin Courtney and Cousin Hillary were pretty and blonde and skinny and that they made Marcie feel like Betty Blimp.

What I couldn't figure out was how Mrs. Winner could be so insensitive. But like Marcie always said, her mother didn't even have a clue about anything.

Sensing she was losing the argument, Marcie switched tactics. "And besides," she said with a crafty look, "you better not leave Ellen alone in the house. She'll go snooping around through the drawers while we're gone."

That certainly got Mrs. Winner's attention. She stopped arguing and turned to stare at me. "I don't really think Ellen would . . ." It was half statement, half question.

"Oh, *yeah*? You watch—she'll go poking around the closets and the desk, looking for your bankbooks and—"

"I would *not*!" I gasped indignantly. "I'd never do such a thing!"

Marcie ignored me. "Remember the housekeeper we had—the skinny one with the big nose?" she continued, all excited now. "Remember Father caught her snooping in—"

"Quite enough, Marcella," Mrs. Winner said hurriedly. Turning to me, she said sweetly, "Actually, Ellen dear, a girl your age should be out, having fun on her day off. Why don't you go to the beach with your friends?"

"Mrs. Winner," I said, clearing my throat, "I don't *know* anybody on Cape Cod." For a smart lady, Thelma Winner could be awfully dense sometimes.

"Yes, well," she said, biting her lip and looking thoughtful, "we'll figure something out, I'm sure."

Right after lunch, the telephone rang. "Ellen

Gardner, please,'' a nasal voice demanded imperiously. ''Lucy Bower calling.''

I had already heard all about poor Lucy Bower, courtesy of Marcie, who loves to make fun of her. Lucy Bower has been with Winner & Winner practically since the firm began. According to Marcie, Lucy is old, ugly, mean, and crabby.

Marcie told me quite proudly she had made up a special nickname for Lucy Bower. ''I call her 'Loose Bowels','' she giggled.

As I listened to Lucy talking away, I kept thinking about Marcie's nickname and I had to bite my cheeks so I wouldn't burst out laughing.

''Mrs. Winner wants to take Marcella and Derek shopping this afternoon,'' Lucy informed me, sounding quite important. ''She wants to get them new outfits and bathing suits for the barbecue Sunday. Please have them cleaned up and ready by 3 o'clock. Mrs. Winner said she'll just toot the horn and—excuse me—what did you say, Mrs. Winner?''

I could hear Mrs. Winner calling something to her and Lucy putting her hand over the receiver. A few seconds later, she came back to the phone. ''Er—Ellen—Mrs. winner would like you to come along shopping, too.''

''Certainly, Miss Bower,'' I said, trying not to laugh, because I knew Mrs. Winner's Game Plan. She was getting paranoid about letting me stay alone in the house.

When I told Marcie about the shopping expedition, she was furious. ''I *hate* going shopping,'' she insisted.

''Who hates going shopping?'' Lisa said gaily as she glided into the kitchen. I hadn't even realized she was in the house, because she was just now, at 1:30 in the afternoon, getting up. ''How can anyone hate shopping?'' she said in a tone of wonder.

''Oh, you,'' Marcie said, giving her a disgusted look. ''You'd shop until you drop.''

Lisa sat down at the table expectantly, as if waiting for me to squeeze the oranges. I ignored her. She gave a pretty little sigh and got up and took the carton of Tropicana out of the refrigerator.

''As long as you and Derek are getting something new to wear for the barbecue, I'll come too,'' Lisa said. ''If I have to go to that barbecue and miss Brandy's pool party, I deserve to get a new outfit.''

''You've got more clothes than any ten girls I know,'' Marcie shot back. Having Lisa come along on the shopping expedition put Marcie in a worse mood than ever. If that was possible. She sulked all the way to the mall.

''I don't want anybody else coming shopping with us,'' she told her mother. ''Just me and you and Derek. Let those two,'' she said, pointing to Lisa and me, ''go by themselves.''

''Very well,'' Mrs. Winner agreed. ''We'll meet Lisa and Ellen in—what do you think, an hour and a half? Right here by the car.'' Off she went, with Marcie grumbling and Derek sucking his thumb as they headed toward Sears.

Lisa whispered to me, ''Sears has a Chubby Shop—that's why Marcie doesn't want us to go with them.'' She shook her beautiful head. ''Oh, I think I would die if I had to buy my clothes in the Chubby Shop.''

''You wouldn't die, Lisa,'' I said, feeling quite annoyed with her. ''You'd just feel pretty awful about everything.'' I didn't feel like telling Lisa I was an ex-chubby. I'm still not as thin as I'd like to be. Once you've shopped in the Pretty-Plus Department, it leaves a scar.

Lisa led the way as we wandered through the small, expensive stores. I had to give her credit—she was a great shopper. But then, she'd had a lot of practice. She knew exactly what to choose. Like the copper-colored silky bathing suit that didn't look like much on the rack but looked fabulous on her body. All the customers stared at her when she came out of the dressing room to get the saleslady's opinion.

She also picked out a raspberry-colored pants outfit, some shorts and a top and a heavy white cotton sweater.

She didn't even glance at the price tags.

I stood watching her, feeling like the Poor Little Match Girl. ''Don't you see anything you like, Ellen?'' she asked, giving a pointed glance at the outfit I was wearing.

I felt like Frances Frump in my faded old jeans and the T-shirt that said, ''PAWTUCKET—THE END OF THE RAINBOW''.

Moving hangers around on the rack with practiced speed, Lisa pulled out an aqua sun dress and held it up to my face. ''This would be great on you,'' she said kindly.

I looked at the price tag and nearly choked. ''Oh wow—I haven't got that kind of money.''

''Well, charge it,'' Lisa said. She had no idea there were people who couldn't afford seventy dollars for a little cotton sun dress.

''I don't have a credit card.''

''You don't have a *credit card*?'' Lisa looked like she was about to go into shock.

I took a deep breath, trying not to let that familiar stab of envy get to me. But it wasn't easy. Especially as I watched the salesclerk carefully wrapping Lisa's purchases. I couldn't believe how much those things cost.

What she had just put on her Visa card would have paid for half of my electronic typewriter. I thought of how hard I had to work for my money, and I started feeling sorry for myself.

Which is why I bought a pair of silver-and-turquoise earrings in the jewelry shop next door. just to make myself feel better.

And also because the saleslady said turquoise was supposed to be lucky. They cost fifteen dollars, which is more than I had ever paid for any jewelry, but if they were going to bring me good luck, they were worth the money.

I decided to wear them home. As soon as I put them on, I had this hunch that something wonderful was going to happen. Maybe Todd would suddenly get interested in me. It changed my whole mood and I felt incredibly happy.

''What are *you* grinning about?'' Marcie scowled at me when we met them at the car. She was in a bad mood, and I could understand why. I remembered those try-on rooms in the Chubby Girls Department and how depressed I used to get trying to find something that looked halfway decent.

Mrs. Winner, at least, was in a fine mood. ''Marcella is all set,'' she told us happily. ''She got a new bathing suit and a lovely pink outfit, didn't you, sweetface. And Derek got some shorts and T-shirts. He's growing like a weed.''

''Weed,'' said Derek. Everyone got all excited because he'd said a brand-new word. Mrs. Winner was so pleased she even broke down and agreed to pick up some pizzas for dinner.

The telephone was ringing as we came into the house. Mrs. Winner rushed over to answer it. ''For you, Ellen dear,'' she trilled.

''For me?'' The only one who would be calling was Mom. Only it wasn't my mother. The voice on the other end was a male voice. Deep, warm, sexy.

''Hello, Ellen,'' he said.

''Who's this?'' I croaked. I didn't dare hope.

''Oh, come on—don't you know?'' A rich, wonderful laugh.

Yes, of course I knew. As I cradled the phone lovingly, my new silver-and-turquoise earrings made a tiny tinkling sound.

My hunch had been right after all.

Those earrings had brought me good luck. The kind of luck I'd been dreaming about.

Todd's voice sounded even better on the telephone than in person.

''Sure,'' I said, ''I know who this is.'' And it was as if there was a little bird singing in my heart.

10

"Ellen," he asked, "do you believe in Destiny?"

Did I? Why else would I have spent fifteen dollars for those good luck earrings. My heart was pounding.

"Because," Todd continued, "I think you and I are destined to get together."

There was a silence. I racked my brain, thinking of something to say. I was so nervous that I had accidentally wrapped the telephone cord around my waist as I paced back and forth.

Suddenly Todd's voice changed. "So—vot's der matter mit you, Ellen? Vy don't you say some-tink?"

"Oh no—it's only *you*," I blurted out. What a terrible letdown. It wasn't Todd Crowley after all.

"For Pete's sake," I snapped, "what do *you* want?" I could feel my face burning with embarrassment.

"Is that supposed to be a pun—for *Pete's* sake?" Pete asked.

Through clenched teeth, I repeated, "What do you want?"

"What do I want?" Pete mused. "What does anybody want? A good job . . . a BMW in the garage—"

Something strange was going on. There was nobody in the kitchen, which was very odd, considering there were two pizzas on the table, getting cold.

"Now, look, Pete, I'm busy," I told him. "To what do I owe the honor of this call?"

"I thought you'd never ask, Miz Gardner. The purpose of this call is to inquire as to whether you have any plans for this coming Sunday."

Oho—so that was it! Out of the corner of my eye, I thought I caught a glimpse of Mrs. Winner's beige linen suit out in the hallway. Of course—it was all a setup.

"Well, now, isn't it a coincidence you should inquire as to my availability this coming Sunday," I said sweetly. "But it happens I do have plans."

"You do?"

"Oh, yes. I plan to go through all the drawers in the house to look for bankbooks. Then afterward, I figured I'd go through all the closets."

It sounded as if Pete were muffling a laugh. "Bravo, bravo," he said. "I thought you might want to go to Craigville Beach this Sunday. I know you haven't been to the beach at all. Want to catch some rays?"

I pulled off my new silver-and-turquoise earrings. So much for the good luck they had brought me! "Do I have any choice in the matter?" I asked him very pointedly.

"I like your spirit," Pete said. "Also your enthsiasm."

For the benefit of my audience out in the hall, I said loudly, "What I simply can't figure out is, how did you know I'd be free on Sunday?"

Pete cleared his throat. "Craigville is considered one of the finest beaches on the Eastern Seaboard. Oh—and I'll take care of bringing the food. If it's not a beach day, we can go to the movies or something.''

''Or something,'' I said. ''See you later, fabricator.''

As I was hanging up the telephone, Mrs. Winner swooped into the kitchen. ''Oh, Ellen dear—did I hear you making plans to go somewhere on Sunday?'' she asked archly. ''I'm *so* pleased.''

Marcie, however, wasn't pleased one bit when she learned abut my plans for Sunday.

''Oh, that's so rotten!'' she cried, stamping her foot. ''Ellen gets to go to the beach and I have to go to that dumb barbecue and eat burned hot dogs.'' She and her mother got into a loud shouting match.

As the two of them argued, in came Mr. Winner from the office. He gave them his sorrowful look and they both became quiet. When he found out why Marcie was upset, Mr. Winner chided her gently in his Ten Commandments voice.

''But Marcie,'' he reminded her, ''you don't even *like* the beach.''

''But I like Pete,'' Marcie retorted, her mouth set in a small, tight line.

After dinner, Mr. and Mrs. Winner went back to their office, Grandma Brill went out to play bingo, and Lisa went to her friend Candy's house, leaving us three—Marcie, Derek and me—alone again for a change. We parked ourselves in the den. Marcie was restless.

''You're *always* reading,'' she said, slapping the book out of my hand. ''What're you reading now?''

I had been reading one of Grandma Brill's sexy romance novels, but I could only imagine what insulting comment Marcie would have about *that*.

So instead I said, "It so happens I am reading a murder mystery."

"Oh yeah—what's it called?"

I put my hand over the title and said, "It's called 'THE LITTLE BRAT MURDER'. It's about this kid who kept annoying people and—"

"Ha-ha. Very funny." Marcie flicked off the TV set. She was in a talkative mood. "I like mysteries and scary stories. Once I saw this movie on TV about a haunted house. I was so scared I had to sleep with my light on."

I looked at her in surprise. It had never occurred to me that Marcie would be afraid of anything. I kept forgetting she was only ten years old.

An idea was dancing around in my head. "You know, Marcie," I began, trying to gauge her reaction, "I know a lot of scary stories. How would you like—oh, no, never mind. Forget it."

"How would I like *what*?"

"No, never mind. Your mother wouldn't like it."

That made Marcie sit up, all right. "I don't care what *she* thinks. Tell me what you were going to say."

I gave an elaborate shrug. "Oh—it's nothing, really. I was just thinking it would be fun to have a Scary Story Party. I could—oh, no, forget I mentioned it. You'd probably get too scared anyhow."

"I wouldn't get scared," she insisted. "You couldn't scare me by telling me some dumb story."

"We-e-ll, all right. Only you have to promise not to tell your mother. She might not like it."

Marcie crossed her heart. "And hope to die," she added. "Derek, too."

"Okay then, let's get the room ready." By now it was about 8:30 p.m., and getting dark outside.

I pulled down the shades and closed the drapes. It was raining lightly and the wind had begun to rise.

I shut off all the lights in the room except for the small, dim lamp in the corner.

I pushed my chair to the darkest corner of the den. Derek, who had been watching everything with interest, suddenly began to whimper.

"Cut that out, you little baby," Marcie told him sternly. She sat back on the sofa in anticipation.

Making my voice low, quivery and sinister, I said, "Welcome to the Theater of Horror. Tonight, I am going to tell you the story of"—here I paused—"THE MASQUE OF THE RED DEATH!"

Derek gave a little shriek and hopped up onto the couch, huddling next to Marcie.

I sat for a moment, collecting my thoughts as I tried to remember all the details of that story. I had read it once maybe three of four years ago when Bobbie-Lou and I were into this thing of reading Poe. Now I couldn't remember a lot of the details. *But what the heck*, I thought to myself, *Marcie wouldn't know if I told it wrong anyhow.*

In my *Twilight Zone* voice, I continued, "Once upon a time, a terrible plague spread across Europe. Throughout the land there was devastation and horror. Skeletons littered the countryside as people died from"—here I made another dramatic pause—"THE RED DEATH!"

Marcie was sitting ramrod-straight as Derek clutched her hand.

"It so happened there was an evil prince who mistreated the poor peasants. He took their lands and crops and starved them. When the evil prince heard the Red Death was coming, he devised a cruel and evil plan—"

A sudden tapping on the window made all three of us jump. It had started to rain heavily and the drops slanted loudly against the windowpanes. The room seemed darker than ever now.

I continued the story. ''And so the prince took all the crops and the food and the drinking water away from the peasants. And he locked all those poor, hungry people out of his castle.'' My voice became a hoarse whisper. ''So the peasants had no hope. For if they did not die of the Red Death, they would starve in the fields.''

''That was rotten,'' Marcie whispered.

''Yes, it was rotten and cruel,'' I said. ''Only the rich lords and ladies were invited to the castle. And night after night, there were feasts and music and dancing as the prince and the nobles waited for the plague to end. And outside the castle, the poor peasants lay dying, without food or water, as the Red Death raged all around.''

Marcie and Derek were breathing loudly.

I was hamming it up and enjoying it. ''Day after day, the peasants would knock at the castle door, begging for food and water, begging to get inside the castle, too, so that they might escape the Red Death. but the prince would not allow the doors to be opened. As he and his rich friends feasted and laughed and danced, they could hear the screams and agony of the people outside.''

''I hate that prince,'' Marcie declared.

I shushed her and went on. ''Then, one night, as the music played and the nobles danced in the ballroom, suddenly there was a knock on the castle door. It was so loud and so ominous that—''

A sudden clap of thunder outside made us shriek. I composed myself. In a low, dramatic voice, I said,

"And suddenly the door flew open. And there stood something so terrifying—so horrible—that everyone stopped dancing and gasped. Never had they seen anything like it."

I sat back, silent.

A moment or two elapsed and then Marcie whispered, "What did they see?"

"I can't tell you the ending. Not tonight. You must wait until the morrow." Marcie started to yell, but I told her, "That's how a Scary Story Party works."

"That's not fair," Marcie started to say, but I silenced her. "TO BE CONTINUED," I declaimed in my quivery voice.

Marcie jumped off the couch and put on the bright overhead light. Derek was sucking his thumb. He had his nightgown wrapped around him.

"That wasn't so scary," Marcie said, but her voice sounded shaky. "I'm hungry," she added. "Let's go in the kitchen." All that story telling had made me hungry, too. I followed her and Derek into the kitchen. "Let me see," Marcie said, opening the refrigerator, "I want something different. Make me a western. Or a fried-egg sandwich."

"Sorry," I said. "I'm off duty. And I'm tired. How about a peanut butter sandwich?"

"I *hate* peanut butter."

"You know something, Marcie?" I said. "I bet those starving peasants out in the fields would have been happy to get a peanut butter sandwich."

Marcie stood there, thinking. I could feel the power rising up within me. "And furthermore, if you bug me about a fried-egg sandwich, you won't get to hear the end of the story tomorrow. It's peanut butter or nothing."

Not even waiting for her reply, I took the big jar of Jif from the cupboard and smeared it on three slices of bread.

Marcie made a face. But she sat down at the table. ''You promise you'll tell us the end of that story tomorrow?''

''If you don't bug me.''

''Well, okay then.'' Marcie poured herself a big glass of milk. ''Yuck—this peanut butter sticks to the roof of my mouth. When I eat peanut butter, I can hardly talk.''

''Really?'' I said. ''In that case, have another sandwich!''

11

It was like watching Perry Mason in action. Only better.

We sat around the kitchen table watching as Mr. Winner paced back and forth, cross-examining Lisa.

"You told us—did you not—that you were driving carefully, Lisa? That you had both hands on the wheel?" He stopped pacing and turned to face Lisa, who was sobbing her heart out.

"But the truth is—you were *not* driving carefully, were you?" Mr. Winner just stood there and looked at Lisa with those sorrowful eyes of his. "Did you, in fact, have both hands on the wheel? Answer yes or no."

Between huge, shuddering sobs, Lisa whispered, "No." Only Lisa could look that good when she cried. If it were me, my nose would be red and swollen and my eyes would disappear. But not Lisa—tears slid gracefully out of her big brown eyes, not even smudging her mascara.

"You left evidence on the front seat," Mr. Winner went on relentlessly. "When the insurance adjuster went to look at the Volvo, he found that evidence."

Here, Mr. Winner looked at each of us intently, as if we were a jury. You could hear a pin drop in the kitchen, except for Lisa's constant sobbing.

"And that evidence was clear and unmistakable." His voice rising, he went on, "Lisa left a slice of pizza on the front seat! And *that* is why she rear-ended the Buick in front of her. Lisa did *not* have both hands on the wheel, as she first claimed."

Thelma Winner chimed in, "I was mortified when the adjuster told me he found that piece of pizza. Obviously, Lisa, you had been driving with one hand and eating with the other."

"Maybe she was hungry," Grandma Brill suggested.

"Oh, stay out of this, Mother," Mrs. Winner said, sounding very annoyed. She stood up, pointed her finger at Lisa, and said, "I don't understand why you left the pizza there. You should have thrown it away as soon as you could. You should have put it in your pocketbook—anything. But you left it there and the adjuster saw it."

"That's because I was nervous," Lisa sniffed.

"It's because you were dumb," Marcie said.

Finally, Mr. Winner pronounced sentence. To teach Lisa responsibility, he was going to punish her. Horror of horrors, Lisa would be grounded the next night, which was Friday. It would be too cruel to ground her on Saturday, and she had to make her big guest-star appearance on Sunday at the Cousins Club barbecue.

Marcie was thrilled to see Lisa, for once, being punished. Only it didn't work out the way Marcie expected. On Friday night, Mr. and Mrs. Winner went out to dinner and Grandma went off to one of her meetings. Half an hour after they left, the doorbell rang, and in marched a bunch of Lisa's friends—Brandy and Mandy or whatever their names were—and some good-looking guys I had never seen before.

Fifteen minutes later, who should show up at the front door but Todd Crowley, with a big pizza from Atsa My Momma.

''Seeing how Lisa never got to finish her pizza when she plowed into that Buick, I thought I'd bring one over for her,'' Todd smiled. Brandy Simms had rushed downstairs and was falling all over him. ''Oh, Toddykins, you are just too, too much! I love it! I hope you got pepperoni on it.''

Marcie stood there watching everything and getting redder by the minute. ''None of you are supposed to be here,'' she shouted. ''Lisa's grounded. I'm gonna tell my mother and father when they get home.''

''Zip your lip, bratkins,'' Brandy told her. ''Nobody said Lisa couldn't have company, did they?''

''Don't you just love that kid?'' Todd said as he followed Brandy upstairs to Lisa's room. The two of them laughed loudly.

I felt like the scullery maid as I sat in the kitchen with Marcie and Derek, trying to ignore the blare of Lisa's stereo and all the laughing and yelling from her room.

The only bright spot of the night was when I decided to bake Crunchy Toffee Squares. Even before they cooled, Marcie started cutting them. ''Hey, wait a minute,'' I told her. ''They're too warm yet.''

''I've got a right,'' Marcie said, ignoring me. ''After all, I stirred the chocolate chips in.''

We could hear Brandy's voice over all the others. Every time she let out a peal of laughter, I thought I would gag.

''These things are good,'' Marcie said as she cut

another big piece. "What do you call them?"

"I call them Marcies," I answered. "On account of they're so nutty."

"Ha-ha. Such a wit." But Marcie seemed pleased. "Here, Derek, here, boy," she called to her brother, as if he were a puppy. "Here's a piece for you. Have a Marcie. They're named after me on account of they're so nice and sweet."

We agreed to save the rest of the toffee squares for the next day. "They taste even better if you let them sit a while," I said. Marcie stood watching me as I cut them out of the baking pan and put them on a plate, covering them with aluminum foil. "Hide them next to the canister," she said. "That way nobody will see them and eat them up."

On Saturday morning, everything hit the fan.

Mrs. Winner was screaming her head off. I had never heard her like that. She had found out that Lisa's friends had come over and partied up in Lisa's room.

"Lisa is grounded for the entire day and night," Mrs. Winner announced. "No visitors. No phone calls. She cannot leave this house until tomorrow when we go to the barbecue."

But that was only the beginning. Derek was running around the kitchen, crying bitterly. "Marcie gone," he howled. "Marcie gone."

"Listen to that," Grandma Brill marveled. "I never heard Derek say Marcie's name before."

Derek kept crying. "Sweetie, Marcie isn't gone," Mrs. Winner said testily. "She's watching TV in the den."

All the crying and hollering must have reached

Marcie's ears, because a second or two later she came racing into the kitchen.

"What happened?" she cried, looking wildly around the kitchen. Her face turned dark red with fury. The blue-and-white plate where I had put the toffee squares was still on the counter, but it was empty, except for a few crumbs.

"The Marcies are gone!" she shrieked. "And I bet Lisa and her dumb friends ate them up. And I put the chocolate chips in myself." She started to cry, too, along with Derek.

"I was going to have some Marcies with milk, right after the cartoons," she sobbed. I had never seen her cry before.

Lisa came into the room. She had heard about being grounded again, and she started crying, too. It was like a concert, with Derek, Marcie, and Lisa all hiccuping and crying.

"If I can't have phone calls and nobody can come over, then what am I supposed to do all night long?" Lisa asked in despair. "How could you make me stay home on a Saturday night?"

"Oh, you'll survive," Mrs. Winner said. "Look at Ellen—I'm certain she sits home plenty of Saturday nights, but she's not crying about it."

"Yes, but Ellen is *used* to it," Lisa whimpered. That Lisa—she really knows how to make someone feel good.

I was so annoyed I decided not to do any ironing the rest of the day. After all, Lisa wouldn't be needing any special outfits just to hang around the house all day and night. We didn't see her for the next few hours, but Marcie reported that she was upstairs crying, giving herself a conditioning treatment and painting her toenails.

Later in the afternoon, we all went food shopping with Mrs. Winner to get some more Nestlé chocolate chips and walnuts so I could make a new batch of toffee squares.

They practically disappeared from the moment they came out of the oven. Even Mr. Winner came back for more. Marcie stuffed herself. "If I don't eat 'em up, somebody else will," she reasoned.

Mr. and Mrs. Winner went out for dinner that night. Grandma Brill made her famous lemon chicken. She brought up a tray to Lisa, who refused to come downstairs.

Finally, about eight o'clock, Lisa emerged from her room, looking bored and sad.

"Ellen, what do you *do* when you stay home on a Saturday night?" she asked. Her voice was quivering.

I had no patience with poor Lisa and her problems. "Whatever. Read. Listen to music. Watch TV. Or," I added, "you could watch the movie your mother rented."

Marcie made a noise like she was pretending to retch. "Yuck. Why does she always rent those goody-goody movies? I wish we had a horror movie instead."

Matter of fact, I wondered about Mrs. Winner's logic. All week long, Marcie and Derek watched anything they wanted to on TV—all kinds of blood and gore and violence. But on the weekend, Mrs. Winner rented movies only if they were "wholesome".

Lisa sat on the edge of the sofa, staring down at her newly painted coral-colored toenails. "I was going to cut Candy's hair tonight," she said sadly. "and then we were all going to a party afterward."

"Oh, you're always giving haircuts and perms to your dumb friends," Marcie said. "Big deal."

"How did you learn to cut hair?" I asked. Lisa actually did give very good haircuts. She also gave a terrific perm to her friend Tammy.

"I like cutting hair," Lisa said. "And giving facials and things. It's fun." She lifted a strand of Marcie's hair. "I wish you'd let me give you a haircut, Marcie. I could do it really nice."

"No *way*. You're not a hairdresser," Marcie replied.

Lisa turned to me. "What about you, Ellen? You could really use a trim."

I was about to tell Lisa I liked my hair long and I was tired of having everyone tell me to get it cut. But then, I remembered how I'd glanced in the mirror that very afternoon and noticed how my hair just seemed to *hang* there.

As if she read my mind, Marcie made an insulting comment about my hair. That settled it. Before I even realized what was happening, I was marching upstairs, ready to have my hair cut and styled by Lisa. "Go wet your head down in the bathroom sink," Lisa told me.

"Yeah," Marcie giggled. "Lisa's right. Go soak your head, Ellen." She and Derek laughed loudly.

Back in the bedroom, Lisa sat me down at her dressing table. She put a towel on my shoulders and combed through my hair. Then she took out her cutting scissors. I told her she looked like a pro.

"Maybe someday I will be," she said very seriously. She sectioned off my hair with clips and started to cut.

Suddenly I felt panicky. "Maybe you—maybe I—you better stop."

"I can't stop now—I've already started cutting. But don't worry," she reassured me. "I'm just taking some hair off the top here . . . this will give you some height . . ."

Lisa continued to snip and clip.

". . . I'm going to layer the sides . . . it's better away from your face." She stepped back for a moment and stared at me. "Ellen," she said in her little voice, "you've got nice eyes. I never noticed them before. They show up so much better with your hair away from your face."

Grandma Brill had shuffled in to watch the Great Beauty Makeover. "That Lisa," Grandma said, beaming. "She's got golden hands."

"If her hands are so golden, how come you don't let her do *your* hair, Grandma?" Marcie asked. "Brandy Simms says your hair looks like a fright wig."

"I will," Grandma promised. "One of these days, you'll see."

"You always say that, Grandma." Lisa sounded hurt. "But you never let me. I could give you a nicer perm than that one. And a nicer hair color, too."

It seemed like an eternity until Lisa finished cutting my hair and started to blow it dry. She twirled the brush around, humming to herself. "A little fullness back here . . . that's good . . . okay, now shut your eyes, everybody. You too, Marcie. Don't anyone look till I'm done."

I shut my eyes tightly. Lisa gave my head a few little pats. Then she told us all to open our eyes. I already had mine open. As if in slow motion, I watched Marcie. She sat there, staring at me.

I had my back to the mirror, so I couldn't see what I looked like.

"Well? What do you think?" Lisa asked. Nobody said a word. I held my breath.

Lisa handed me a little mirror. "You can see how the back looks," she said. Before I could even glance in the mirror, I knew the verdict as soon as Marcie spoke.

All she said was, "Okay—now cut *my* hair."

12

''You look different,'' Pete said when he picked me up the next morning. ''What did you do?''

''I didn't do anything. It was Lisa—she cut my hair.''

''Well, it looks great. I like it.'' Pete opened the door of his truck and helped me in.

We rode in silence for a while, mostly because I felt funny being with him. After all, Mrs. Winner had arranged the whole thing. And when I saw the sign on Pete's truck that said ''YARD WORK AND VERY ODD JOBS'', it made me feel rotten. I mean, I wasn't thrilled to be thought of as just another very odd job.

''So,'' Pete said after a few minutes, ''what time are the Winners leaving for their barbecue?''

''Probably as soon as I walked out the front door,'' I laughed. ''And anyway, how did *you* know they were going to a barbecue? I never told you.''

''Ellen, I know everything that goes on in that house. Don't forget—my family has known the Winners from the time they moved down to the Cape.''

''Tell me about the Winners,'' I said, making myself comfortable on the seat. ''I'd like to have somebody tell *me* a story for a change.''

As we drove to the beach, Pete told me the saga

of Martin and Thelma Winner, starting with when they were poor, struggling lawyers starting up their law practice.

"My mother used to baby-sit Lisa after school," Pete said. "A lot of the time the Winners couldn't even afford to pay her."

I listened, fascinated, as Pete told the story of how Martin Winner changed his image and his luck. "The way my father tells it, Mr. Winner was a skinny, ordinary guy with short hair and kind of a high voice. Anyhow, he got contact lenses, let his hair grow long, and then took some kind of course. It was either public speaking or some kind of assertiveness thing. Anyhow, that's what really changed his image. After that, he had that Bible-movie voice."

I digested that information. "It's nice to know Mr. Winner is an ordinary mortal like the rest of us," I said. "So how did he become such a hotshot lawyer?"

"I'm coming to that," Pete said. "Okay—here's Martin Winner with this new look and new voice. And then one day, somebody referred a case to him—a fisherman who'd gotten hurt on a fishing boat. And what do you think happened?"

I shook my head. "What happened," Pete continued, "is that Mr. Winner went in front of the jury with his totally new image and his totally new voice, and he got that fisherman the biggest settlement anyone had ever been awarded in Massachusetts. That case made legal history. The Boston papers even wrote it up—they said Mr. Winner had the entire jury crying."

"I can believe that," I agreed. "I've seen him in action. What about Mrs. Winner—is she a trial lawyer, too?"

"No," said Pete, "but they say she's the brains

behind everything. She branched out into estate planning and probate and money matters. That's her specialty. So with all the people retiring to Cape Cod the last few years, she has plenty of clients, too.'' A grin broke over his face. ''Between Mr. Winner with his jury trials and Mrs. Winner with the senior citizens, they've got 'em coming and going.''

''So Winner & Winner hit the big time,'' I concluded. ''And everybody lived happily ever after.''

Pete raised his eyebrow, noting the sarcasm in my voice. ''Except for Marcie and Derek,'' he said, ''Those kids got shortchanged.''

''You're right,'' I agreed. ''Sometimes I think Mr. and Mrs. Winner know more about their clients than they do about their kids.''

''Very astute observation,'' Pete said. ''Matter of fact, somebody I know said those exact words once to Mrs. Winner. Her excuse was she didn't have time because she worked all day.''

''That's no excuse,'' I said hotly. ''Look at my mom—she works all day, too, sometimes overtime and Saturday mornings. And she doesn't have help in the house, except for me. But she's never been too busy to help me or to listen or to . . . and she brought me up all alone and . . .'' My voice trailed off. Thinking about Mom gave me a lump in my throat.

''And she did a darn good job, too.'' Pete gave me an awkward pat on the hand. ''Was it lonely being an only child?''

I thought about that for a moment. ''Not really *lonely*,'' I said slowly. ''More like *lonesome* at times. I mean, I always used to wish I had a brother or sister.''

"Look at the bright side. You could have had a sister like Marcie."

We both started to laugh. "You know something, Pete?" I said, feeling more and more comfortable with him. "The funny thing is, I would have *sworn* that if you lived in a beautiful house, and you had money, and your parents weren't divorced, and you had a brother and sister, you'd *have* to be happy. But I guess it doesn't always work out that way, does it."

"Things don't always work out the way you figure," Pete said softly.

By now we were close to the beach and I could smell the ocean. "This is great," I said, taking a deep breath of fresh salt air. "Do you realize this is the very first time I've been to the beach since I got to Cape Cod?"

Craigville Beach was already quite crowded as we walked across the hot sand, looking for a place to spread the blanket.

"This is the life," I sighed, kicking off my thongs and unzipping my terry-cloth beach shift. "I give this day a 10—it's perfect."

The beach looked as if it went on forever. The sun sparkled on white-capped, blue-green waves as they pounded on the long expanse of clean white sand.

I lent Pete my Bain de Soleil, and we smeared ourselves with it, then lay down on the blanket. It was nice being able to relax and listen to the sound of the waves and not have to worry about what Marcie and Derek were up to. And it was relaxing being with Pete—I didn't have to worry about making conversation like I would have if he had been a real date.

If he'd been Todd, for instance. Thinking about Todd made me sit up and wipe the sweat from my forehead. "This sun is pretty strong," I said to Pete. "I think it's about time to go in the water."

"I'll join you," Pete said. He stood up, then pulled me up. We walked down to the water's edge, the sand burning the soles of our feet.

"Take it slow," Pete said, but I felt so sweaty I just ran into the water—then let out one loud shriek.

"Brrrr. It's like ice." I ran back to where Pete was standing.

"I told you to take it slow, a little at a time," he said. "This is your first time in the water this summer."

The two of us went in slowly. Pete was right. It was a lot easier that way. There were a lot of waves, and around us people were jumping and hollering every time a big wave hit. Pete took my hand and we did some wave jumping for a while. Then I realized I was starving.

It was a long walk back to the blanket. Pete was still holding my hand, and I wasn't sure whether or not to pull it away. I did, but not until we sat down and began drying ourselves off with towels.

"Let's see what we've got here," Pete said, opening the cooler. "My sister Susan packed the lunch." I had expected peanut butter and jelly, but instead there was thin-sliced roast beef on rolls, ice-cold grapes and plums, plus the best lemon cookies I'd ever tasted.

"Sue thought up the recipe for these cookies," Pete said. "She's going to enter it in the Pillsbury Bake-Off." He poured me some more lemonade.

Even after a sandwich and three cookies, I was

still hungry. Pete had been lying on his elbow, staring at me. "You have the best appetite of any girl I ever knew," he said.

I felt embarrassed.

"Hey—I didn't mean it that way," Pete said. "I think it's terrific to see a girl who really enjoys her food."

"I think that's what they call a left-handed compliment," I told him. I finished another sandwich and had one more cookie. Then we cleaned up the things from lunch, put on more Bain de Soleil, and stretched out again, turning over to tan our backs.

"I feel like an old cat," I told Pete contentedly. "I'm so nice and relaxed I could fall asleep."

"That's not much of a compliment to me. I was hoping you were feeling all excited," he said.

"Actually, I am. That's why I ran into the water—to cool off. Otherwise I would have attacked you."

"I'm glad you restrained yourself," he teased.

"It took a lot of self-control," I said, and we both started to laugh. We lay on the blanket for a few minutes, shoulders touching. It felt kind of nice. But then I opened one eye and looked at Pete's arm. Oh drats—it had reddish-blond hairs. For the hundredth time, I thought to myself, *Too bad Pete has red hair!*

Later on we went for a stroll along the beach. Little kids were digging in the sand, old people sat under beach umbrellas, and lots of good-looking guys flirted with girls with deep tans.

One of the guys reminded me of Todd. Without thinking I said, "Does Todd Crowley work in the summer, or what?"

"Can't get him out of your mind, huh?" Pete gave

me a sideways smile. "From what I hear, I don't think Todd's doing much of anything this summer. He was a lifeguard for a while but he quit. Sometimes he helps out in his father's stores."

Just then we saw a group of people starting a volleyball game. "Hey, Pete, I feel like playing." I kind of surprised myself. Usually I would have been too shy to approach a bunch of people I didn't know. But here on Cape Cod, I didn't feel shy. The good part of not knowing anyone was that if I made a fool out of myself, so what?

I must say, I played a good game. Volleyball is one of my favorite sports. I used to love playing it in gym.

"Nice game," Pete said approvingly afterwards. "You are a woman of many talents."

We went into the water again, got some more sun, and then Pete announced, "That's enough sunshine for you today. You're getting too red." We folded up the blanket and carried our things to the truck.

On the way back, Pete showed me the local points of interest. Like the Craigville Conference Center, where they have the Cape Cod Writers' conferences, and the Hyannis Melody Tent. He also pointed out the first house the Winners lived in, before they became successful.

Then he showed me the major point of interest. "Now this place," he explained, "is called Passion Alley. You should see the cars here on Saturday night—it's like the world's biggest parking lot."

He turned to me with a make-believe leer and rasped, "Someday, dollink, if you're nice to me, I vill take you to dis place."

I burst out laughing. "What an enticing offer. How could anybody refuse?"

We drove around some more, and then Pete pulled into the parking lot of a place called Seafood by Salty's. As he shut off the ignition, he said, "I bet you've never tasted seafood like they serve here."

Pete was right. It was the best seafood I'd ever had. I ordered the "Seafood Medley With Lobster", and I didn't even care that it was one of the most expensive items on the menu. I figured, since Mrs. Winner was probably paying for it, I might as well go first-class.

Pete pretended to faint when I gave the waitress my order. "And here I thought she was going to be a cheap date," he said.

I finished the meal with a chocolate parfait, which was a la carte. "She can't help it—she's from Rhode Island," Pete told the waitress, who kept making dumb remarks about where I was putting all that food.

After dinner, the two of us started getting silly. I was tired from all that sunshine and fresh air and I was feeling relaxed and full of lobster and ice cream. We started to make up crazy jokes about the Winners, as if they were performers with rock groups. I don't even remember how it all started, but one thing led to another. I made up a joke about Marcie as featured performer with "Marcie and the Brats". Then Pete thought up one for Mrs. Winner—"Thelma and the Tightwads".

"That woman hates to part with a penny," he said. "It kills her to have to pay me decent money, but she doesn't have any choice. It's hard to get help on Cape Cod."

I thought about that and sighed. "If I'd known that, I would have asked for more money."

We went back to thinking up some more rock

groups. I came up with "Derek and the Late Bloomers".

"What about Lisa?" Pete asked. We thought for a few seconds and then decided on "Lisa and the Shoppers".

We couldn't think of one for Mr. Winner, until Pete came up with "Martin and the Disciples." By then, the two of us were laughing hysterically.

"Don't forget Grandma Brill," I said. "But I feel guilty joking about her, the poor thing. What could we call her group?"

"Grandma and the . . ." Pete frowned in concentration. "How about . . .'Grandma and the Whatchamacallits.' "

We laughed all the way home. "You know," I told Pete, "all in all, I didn't have too bad of a time today. I mean, I would have probably had a lot more fun at the Winner Cousins Club. But going to the beach wasn't all that bad."

It was nearly seven o'clock by the time we pulled up in front of the house. Marcie was sitting on the top step of the front porch. Derek was playing on the sidewalk, stepping on ants.

By the scowl on her face, Marcie was not very happy about my going to the beach with Pete.

"Hey, there, Marcie-ola, I like your hair," Pete said, giving her nose a little tweak. "I heard your sister gave you a haircut last night. Looks good that way."

"It really does," I agreed. Lisa had cut Marcie's hair so it hugged her head. It didn't look nearly as frizzy as before.

Bur Marcie was in no mood for flattery. "How come you're so late?" she demanded, looking only at Pete.

Before he could say a word, Grandma Brill poked her head out of the front door. ''Oh, yoo-hoo, Ellen,'' she called, ''What's His Name phoned you about 20 minutes ago—you know who I mean . . .''

''She means Turd Crawling,'' Marcie said.

''Todd called me?'' I could barely get the words out. ''Why? What did he want?''

''Who knows? Who cares?'' Marcie shrugged. ''Anyhow, he's gone out somewhere. If you'd of come back early, you'd of been here when he called.''

Suddenly my good mood left. I felt depressed. All I could think, over and over, was *if only.*

If only I'd left the beach sooner . . . if only I hadn't ordered lobster which took so long . . . if only I hadn't sat in the restaurant so long, joking around.

If only I hadn't been with Pete, I would have been home when Todd Crowley finally called.

13

Monday nite, July 15

Dear Bobbie-Lou,

Hooray! I finally got a letter from you!! It's about time. It sounds like you're having about as much fun down there as I am up here (which isn't much!). Loved the part about your cousins calling you a Damn Yankee! Poor thing—you just can't win.

Before I forget—next time you write, PLEASE DO NOT MENTION MARCIE'S NAME. I *KNOW* she steamed your letter open. The back of the envelope was a mess and it had Scotch tape on it.

I am writing you from the upstairs bathroom. I have to sit here sometimes just to get some privacy. Back to Marcie again—she's been acting very funny toward me ever since Pete took me to the beach yesterday. I think she is up to no good. Anyhow, when I got back I found Todd Terrific had called me. Naturally, I wasn't home. Can you believe that rotten luck of mine?

So I went to the phone to call him and when I picked up the receiver, who should I hear but Marcie. She was playing one of her cute little telephone tricks—calling up different cab companies and telling them to come to Todd's house. I don't know how many cabs she called, but it looked like Taxicab Town next door. The housekeeper was furious. When I confronted Marcie afterward, she denied everything!

And if that isn't bad enough, last night when my mom called, I heard this funny sound on the phone, like somebody breathing hard into the receiver. I told her to hang on and then I tiptoed into the den. There was Marcie—listening in on the extension. I mean, is she rotten or what?

Anyhow, my mom wants to come down for the day in a week or two. I can't wait to see her. I really miss her. I don't think I appreciated her until I met Mrs. W.

Oh, I forgot to tell you. This afternoon Lisa told me why Todd had called—he was inviting me to some party—they didn't have enough girls. DO YOU BELIEVE MY ROTTEN LUCK?????

I hope you are having better luck with guys. How is that friend of your cousin's, the one that's real shy. See if you can draw him out of his shell (you can do it).

Well, y'all, time to sign off. Derek just knocked on the door—he wants me to read to him. Please write soon.

Your hardworking, bad-luck friend,

P.S. Did I ever tell you how I can never get the chance to sit outside and work on a tan? Marcie knows I like to be out in the yard from 1 to 3, so for spite she makes sure I stay in the house doing something until maybe 4:30, when there's hardly any sun. Well, I got this idea about how to keep her busy around that time. What I need is for you to . . .

Monday nite, 7/15

Hi, Mom—

Just a quick note to tell you I really wasn't yelling at Marcie because she listened in when you called me yesterday—I was just joking around with her. Ha-ha. The reason I sounded down in the dumps, like you said, is because I missed a phone call yesterday from this gorgeous guy who lives next door because I was at the beach.

Oh, I do have something nice to tell you. I found out Grandma Brill belongs to a Writers' Group & she said I can sit in on their next meeting, which is going to be at the house. Isn't that great?

Love & XXXX,
Ellen

P.S. Remember that book of horror stories Bobbie-Lou gave me. Is it still in the house? If you get a chance, could you mail it to me here?

14

"You're letting in all the flies," Grandma Brill told Marcie. "You should try to be more careful."

All morning long, Marcie and Derek had been going in and out of the house, banging the screen door loudly. Pete was working in the yard, which is the only reason Marcie ever went outside.

I was busy putting dishtowels away when I overheard Marcie and Grandma Brill arguing.

"Those grape Popsicles aren't good for you," Grandma was saying earnestly. "You should eat healthy things—like fruit or juice."

Marcie pulled the paper off and took a big bite. "Oh, sure," she said, "grape Popsicles are junk, but I suppose prune juice Popsicles are just fine."

"Prune juice Popsicles?" Grandma Brill blinked. "They have prune juice Popsicles now? I didn't know that."

"Aha!" Marcie sneered. "Prune Popsicles are fine but grape Popsicles are junk, huh? How come? Answer that one."

"But I never said—I didn't even know they had . . . " Her glasses winking and blinking in the late morning sun, Grandma Brill kept turning from Marcie to me.

"Oh, yes you did too, Grandma," Marcie kept on. "Ellen heard you. Didn't you, Ellen?"

I hurried out of the kitchen back to the laundry

room, where I had spent most of the morning. I didn't feel like being a referee in one of Marcie and Grandma's arguments.

Grandma Brill came into the laundry room, shaking her orange curls, and blowing her nose into a paper towel. "Oh, why does she—no matter what I say . . ." she sniffled. "It's terrible—I try to be nice and that child never . . ." Poor Grandma. I didn't know what to say so I went over and hugged her.

Grandma's eyes filled up again. "You're a nice—I'm glad you're here . . ." She composed herself and said, "Why don't you go outside with the children, Ellen. I'll finish the folding."

I had to chuckle to myself. Grandma Brill has this strange sense of timing. Whenever I'm just about finished with something, there she is—offering to help. Now that I'd finished folding three loads of laundry, there she was, coming to my rescue.

I thanked her and headed outside, glad to be in the fresh air. It was a good day to work on my tan, a perfect day actually. The sun was strong but there was enough breeze so you could lie on your back without sweating.

I flopped down on a lounge chair not far from where Marcie and Derek were sitting on the grass, watching Pete trim the hedges.

Marcie was not happy to see me. "How come you're out here?" she asked. "Wherever I go, you're always creeping around."

Pete started to laugh. "Now Marcie, who wouldn't want to hang around with you? You're terrific company."

"That's the price you have to pay for being such a fun person," I told Marcie.

She shot me a furious glance, then turned away and started talking and giggling with Pete. As if I cared.

Derek came over and tapped my shoulder. He had his book of nursery rhymes and pointed to his favorite page, ''Bobby Shaftoe''. I started reading it to him.

> ''. . . Bobby Shaftoe's gone to sea
> Silver buckles on his knee . . .''

''Hey, Derek,'' Marcie called to him. ''I know a good nursery rhyme. Want to hear it?''

Derek nodded and Marcie walked over toward us. ''Okay, it goes like this,'' she said loudly:

> ''Mary had a bicycle
> Made out of solid glass,
> And every time she hit a bump
> A piece went up her–''

''Marcie!'' I yelled.

She looked at me, all innocence. ''I was just going to say, 'A piece went up her dress.' What's wrong with that?''

With that, Marcie began to giggle. ''C'mere, Derek–I want to talk to you.''

Derek trotted off, and I turned my lawn chair in the direction of the sun. I wanted to keep up the tan I'd gotten Sunday at the beach.

''Hey, Ellen,'' Pete stood over me, ''we're planting some flowers back there for Marcie. Want to help? Or keep us company?''

''Her?'' Marcie snorted. ''Ellen's scared to death

of worms. You might dig one up and then she'd probably die."

"You got that right," I agreed. "Just looking at worms makes me sick. I'd die if I ever touched one."

I adjusted my chair and lay back. I was wearing shorts and a T-shirt, so I ran the risk of getting an uneven tan, but it was better than nothing.

The sun was getting stronger. I shut my eyes, listening to the hum of voices and the clink of Derek's pail and shovel. It was making me sleepy. Derek came over to me.

"El," he said. His curly head brushed against my hand.

"No more reading now," I said drowsily.

Derek touched my arm. "Whirr," he said.

"Whirr," I repeated. The sound made me even sleepier.

From the kitchen, I could hear Grandma clanking dishes. The sounds of summer made me feel so relaxed and happy. Horseflies droned, screen doors opened, cars drove leisurely down Harbor Road.

I daydreamed about Todd:

Todd could hardly take his eyes off Ellen, who looked marvelous with her glowing tan and her silver-and-turquoise earrings.

"You look fantastic," he said. Ever so gently, he reached out and caressed her arm . . ."

"Whirr," Derek kept saying in his sweet little voice. The sun had gotten very strong and I could feel beads of sweat trickling down my body.

But no—it was more like a *crawling* sensation on my arm.

I sat up. At first I couldn't figure out what it was, because there was a film of sweat around my eyes. But then I saw it.

I screamed. And screamed. And kept on screaming! Winding its way across my arm up toward my shoulder was a long, pink worm.

I shouted and sobbed as I threw it off my arm. And I screamed even louder when I saw the other worm that was on my leg.

Pete came racing over and pulled two more wriggling worms off the lounge near my feet. And, oh, grossest thing of all, there was half a worm near where my head had been. "Get them away," I hollered over and over.

Derek stood there with his little pail. There was a worm crawling over the edge of the pail. Derek burst out crying, too. "Whirr," he sobbed. "Whirr."

"It was Marcie," I screamed. "That rotten little brat put him up to it!"

Tears were rolling down my face and I was shuddering and shaking. Pete turned me around, looked me over, and said, "You're okay. They're all gone."

Marcie was nowhere to be seen and Derek was still crying. "It's all right," Pete told him. "You didn't mean any harm, Derek. Ellen's not mad at *you*."

Pete helped me up the stairs. I ran through the kitchen past Grandma Brill, who stared at me open-mouthed. Still whimpering, I ran into the bathroom and locked the door. Then I ripped off my clothes and took the longest, hottest shower I'd taken since I got there. I scrubbed my hair, my face, my entire body. In all my life I had never felt so awful and slimy.

When I finally came downstairs my hair was still dripping wet. Marcie was sitting at the kitchen table, eating lunch and talking to Pete. She didn't look at me as I came in.

"I want to know why," I said to Pete. "Why did she do that?"

Marcie took a big gulp of soda and burped loudly. "Ellen is a big baby. It was just a little joke."

I sat down and stared at Marcie until she had to look up at me. Her eyes darted around like a Ouija Board. She couldn't look me in the eye.

"Here's another joke, then," I said. "Remember tonight I was supposed to tell you the ending of *The Dancing Skeleton*?"

Marcie bit her cuticle and nodded. "Remember when I left off, the skeleton came in and woke up the little kid?"

Again Marcie nodded.

"Well, I am *never* going to tell you the ending. And if you pull any more tricks like the one you just pulled, I'll never tell you another story. That's it."

Marcie sucked in breath. "That's rotten. And anyhow, I don't care. I'll find out the end of the story myself."

"Oh, no, you won't!" I crowed. "You'll never know—because that's *my* story—I thought it up and I'm the only one that knows the answer!"

"You're the meanest mother's helper we ever had," Marcie cried hotly.

I leaned toward her. "All your life—even when you're an old lady, you'll sit in your rocking chair and wonder: 'Gee, I wonder what happened to that little kid that night the dancing skeleton came in.' And you'll never know. Because I wrote that story and I'm going to be a famous writer some day."

Marcie sat there gaping at me. She didn't say a word.

Later on, before he left, Pete took me aside. "You got me curious," he said. "What *did* happen? How does that story end?"

"How the heck should I know?" I shrugged. "I make up those dumb endings as I go along. I don't even know how it ends myself!"

15

VR-OOO-MM. Stop. VR-OOO-MMM. Stop. VR-OOO-MMMMMM

The sound of a vacuum cleaner going on and off, on and off, woke me up the next morning. I looked at the clock radio and saw it was still early.

Who would be running a vacuum cleaner so early in the morning?

There was no way I could sleep with that noise, so I jumped out of bed and headed into the shower. When I came downstairs, the vacuum was still going strong. I went to see who it was that had this sudden urge to houseclean.

To my surprise, there in the living room was a thin, very pretty black girl wearing a head set and earphones. As she ran the vacuum cleaner, she would do little dance steps, then shut the cleaner off. I noticed she had on a really sharp-looking outfit—gold-colored slacks with a gold-and-white top. As I stood watching her, she turned and smiled at me.

I smiled back and went into the kitchen, figuring the whole family would be up by now because of the noise. But the only one in the kitchen was a heavyset black woman, nearly six feet tall and wearing a muumuu. She had gold hoop earrings and a bunch of gold chains around her neck. Now, I am by no means an expert on jewelry, but all that gold looked real. And expensive.

"Look at this mess," she grumbled to herself. "In one week they slopped everything up." What looked like a big diamond ring sparkled on her finger as she moved with lightning speed, wiping down the chairs and the table.

I stood there, not sure what to say or do. She glanced at me, shook her head, and continued complaining. "Why I even *bother* coming round here, I don't know. There's no *order* in this house—no *decorum*!"

Derek came into the kitchen, followed by Marcie, who let out a happy shriek.

"Julienne—you're back! Did you have a nice time?' Marcie tried to hug her, but the woman gave her a make-believe push.

"Now don't you come acting all sweet and innocent around *me*, girl. I saw the mess you made in the den—everything's all sticky from them purple Popsicles." With that, Julienne snapped the cleaning cloth against Marcie's arm.

"Hey—that hurts!" Marcie yelped, but she didn't seem upset.

"And furthermore, you better not make a mess around here when you fix breakfast," the woman warned.

"*I* don't have to fix breakfast. *She's* supposed to." Marcie pointed to me and made a face. "She's the new mother's helper, but she's not much help."

"You hush up now," Julienne said, practically punching the refrigerator as she wiped it. "That's no way to talk to anybody. If there was any decorum in this house, you wouldn't be needing no mother's helpers and such."

Marcie looked at me puzzled. "Hey, Ellen, what does 'decorum' mean?"

"Hah," Julienne cried triumphantly. "See that? If you got to ask what it is, you ain't got any."

Marcie didn't answer. She got up meekly, went to the cupboard and took out the box of cereal. Then she got three bowls and spoons and actually served breakfast to Derek and me.

I knew it was just to impress Julienne.

Suddenly I remembered why that name rang a bell. It was on the inscription in Derek's nursery-rhyme book. Julienne had given him the book for a Christmas present.

While Marcie and Derek ate their cornflakes, I tried to make conversation. 'That's a pretty name—Julienne," I began. "How do you spell it?"

Her mouth full of cornflakes, Marcie started to answer, "It's J—U—L—"

"She did *not* ask you!" Julienne snapped. Turning to me, she said, "It's spelled J—U—L—I—E—N—N—E."

"It's different," I said. "I never knew anyone with that name before."

Julienne merely grunted as she wiped the stove.

For the sake of having someone to talk to, I babbled on. "Julienne is a French word actually. I mean, I remember it, because we had to look up definitions in English Vocabulary last year. Julienne means to cut something up in small, even matchlike sticks, like julienne carrots or julienne zucchini or—"

"Say what?" Julienne was gawking at me like I had lost my mind.

Marcie started to snicker and I felt like a fool. Well, so much for my morning chitchat. Just then the girl who had been vacuuming came into the kitchen and sat down at the table with us. She told me she was Julienne's niece, Nedra, from upstate New York. Nedra was staying with Julienne for the summer. In the fall, she would be going to Brandeis College.

"Brandeis is a Jewish college," Julienne said proudly. She was starting to warm up a little. "You've got to be real smart to go to a Jewish school. And Nedra got a scholarship there too."

It was nice talking to Nedra. I found out she was planning to be a political science major, and she loved spending the summers on Cape Cod, and that Auntie Julienne and Uncle Ty had taken her and her younger sister with them to Acapulco. They had just gotten back the day before. "I always get jet lag when I travel," Nedra said, yawning as she spoke.

Now *that* was certainly unusual. I mean, how many cleaning women go on vacation to Acapulco? Not to mention taking along two nieces, all expenses paid. And according to Nedra, Auntie Julienne and Uncle Ty loved to travel. They'd been to Europe, Hawaii, the Caribbean, South America, and Hong Kong.

As Nedra and I finished a leisurely breakfast, Julienne handed me a note Mrs. Winner had left for me.

"Oh, that woman!" Nedra shook her head. "She sure is one for writing notes. You should see the one she left for my aunt. I broke up when I read it."

The note, scribbled on Winner & Winner interoffice memorandum paper, read:

TO: Ellen
FROM: THELMA WINNER
SUBJECT: Ironing

Mr. Winner and I had an early meeting in Boston this morning. I did, however, want to remind you that the ironing is piling up. Would you, therefore, take care of it as time permits.

I stuck the note up on the refrigerator. "In case I should forget to do the ironing, this'll remind me," I said.

Nedra giggled. Julienne didn't answer, but as I headed to the laundry room, I thought I heard her mumble something about "decorum".

As I waited for the iron to heat up, Nedra came in with a little pink transistor radio. "Auntie thought you'd like to have some music," she said kindly.

Around 2 o'clock Julienne and Nedra finished cleaning. Julienne had offered to drop me off at the library. I was going to return some books for Grandma Brill, who said her feet hurt too much to walk around the library.

"My bunions are killing me," Grandma moaned. "I can't even get my Reeboks on." Usually she wore a pair of white canvas Reeboks with big holes cut out on the sides. She said that was to relieve the pressure on her bunions.

Poor Grandma limped around the house barefoot. Her bunions looked red and swollen.

"Oh, gross," Marcie said, bending down to get a better look at Grandma's feet. "Ugh—those bunion things are disgusting. They remind me of boobs. It's like you got a pair of boobs on your feet."

I was thrilled to be getting out of the house and away from Marcie for a while. But Marcie made a surprise announcement. "I want to go to the library, too," she decided.

"Since when?" Julienne demanded, hands on

hips. "You're not one for reading books."

"Since now," Marcie said stubbornly. "Ellen always gets to go places. Me and Derek want to go, too."

I tried to talk Marcie out of it. "Are you sure you want to go? It's a long walk back to the house—and you don't like to walk."

But when Marcie makes up her mind, there's no arguing with her.

Julienne, on her way to change out of her muumuu, warned, "Now, Marcie, if you're coming in my car, you better get cleaned up. I don't want any sticky hands. And clean up your brother too."

It was amazing how Marcie obeyed Julienne. About ten minutes later, Marcie and Derek came downstairs looking scrubbed and presentable.

When we got outside to Julienne's car, I saw why she was so fussy. I couldn't believe my eyes.

Julienne drove a highly polished silver Mercedes with pale gray upholstery.

I climbed into the car with my mouth hanging open. I mean, a Mercedes is not the usual means of transportation for most cleaning women. But then, Julienne, as she slid behind the wheel of the Mercedes, certainly didn't look like a cleaning woman, especially now that she had changed into a cream-colored linen outfit. With her gold chains and the big ring sparkling on her well-manicured hands, she looked like a well-to-do lady.

There was a story there somewhere. I made a mental note to ask Pete or Grandma Brill what it was.

Julienne dropped the three of us off in front of the library, with an admonition: "Act nice now—you hear?" Nedra waved good-bye to us. Marcie marched into the library, with Derek trotting shyly behind her.

It was a nice little library. Of course, I happen to like all libraries. Over the checkout counter there was a bulletin board that told about the summer reading program for kids. "You ought to enter that, Marcie," I suggested.

"You ought to bug off," she said loudly. The library aide looked up at her, surprised.

I quickly steered the two of them to the Children's Book section. Derek spotted some picture books at a little table nearby and was completely entranced. He sat down and smiled as he leafed through the books. "Boo," he said happily over and over. "Nice boo."

Marcie, however, was bored. She roamed around, looking irritable. "I don't know why I ever came here," she muttered, as if I had begged her to come along.

I went back to the Current Fiction display and picked up a couple of books there, plus a mystery and a romance novel for Grandma Brill. Then I rejoined Marcie to help her find a book.

It wasn't easy. She said no to *Heidi, Little Women*, and even the Nancy Drew books. "I don't like those girlie things," she said, making a sound of disgust. So I suggested *Robinson Crusoe* and *Treasure Island*. She decided they sounded all right.

I also checked out some books for Derek, who was so happy he kept jumping up and down. Everyone at the library seemed happy to see us leave.

Just as I expected, Marcie complained all the way home. It was hot, it was a long walk, she was thirsty, she was tired. Etcetera.

As we turned the corner near the Winner house, we saw Todd jogging slowly up the street toward us. He stopped and smiled. ''Well, well—if it isn't the Two Little Winners and—''

''And the big Loser,'' Marcie finished the sentence smartly.

Todd eyed my library books. ''Looks like you're planning to do a lot of reading.''

I nodded, wishing I had some sharp comeback. But all I could think of to reply was, ''Uh—do you read a lot?''

''. . . Ah, yes—I love to read,'' Todd confided. ''I knew when I first saw you, we would be soul mates. We love literature and poetry and—''

''Who, me?'' Todd's smile widened. ''The only thing I like to read is T-shirts.''

Fantasy-wise, I was way off lately.

16

On Friday morning, Marcie made her Bombshell Announcement.

"Guess what," she said. "I'm going away for the weekend."

"You're *what*?" I pretended to faint into the pile of sheets I was about to wash. "Oh, no—how will I ever *manage* without you around?"

At first I thought she was kidding, but Mrs. Winner confirmed the good news: Marcie was going to spend the weekend at Grandma Brill's apartment.

Now that was an even bigger surprise, because I never knew Grandma even *had* an apartment. But I learned she's had her little one-bedroom place for a few years now.

"I only call on Mother when I need her," Mrs. Winner said. So far, since I'd been on Cape Cod, Grandma had spent every waking moment at the Winner house.

The idea of Marcia and Grandma Brill spending a weekend together was Mrs. Winner's brilliant idea. "I sense that Marcella is jealous of the closeness between Lisa and my mother," Mrs. Winner told me very seriously. "So I thought if Marcella were to spend the weekend at her grandmother's it would be good."

"Oh, yes," I agreed. Well, it would certainly be good for *me*.

Right after breakfast on Saturday, Marcie and Grandma left. I had helped Marcie pack her little red patent leather suitcase. "We're gonna go out to this fancy place for lunch and go to the movies and everything," she bragged. "We're gonna have a blast."

I thought Derek would be upset after Marcie left, but he was his usual merry little self. I read to him for a while and then we played a couple of games of Memory. Derek is really good at that game—he remembers where all the cards are.

After lunch, I took him for a walk past Todd's house. I had seen Todd's car in the driveway and figured maybe he'd come out of his house as we passed by, but no such luck. I even stopped twice, pretending I had to tie Derek's shoelaces, and I took a long time doing it.

But still no sign of Todd. Once more, Derek and I strolled around the block.

It was a nice afternoon, the kind of day for walking, not staying inside. Derek loved being out of doors. He kept smiling and pointing to everything he saw—flowers growing in a yard, a baby being wheeled in a stroller, a fluffy dog peering at us from behind a fence.

"Daw," cried Derek all excited. "Daw." I wondered how come Mrs. Winner never got a pet for Derek and Marcie.

The two of us walked by Todd's house one last time, swinging hands, as I recited:

"Bobby Shaftoe's fat and fair
Combing down his golden hair,
He's my love forever more
Pretty Bobby Shaftoe . . ."

Derek looked up at me, his cheeks glowing and his eyes full of trust. I just had to hug him. ''You are the best little kid in America,'' I said, and Derek positively glowed. I never saw a kid who enjoyed being hugged so much, but hardly ever got any hugs from his parents.

When we got back to the house, Pete was waiting for us.

''Mrs. Winner told me the big news about Marcie going away for the weekend,'' he greeted us. ''This calls for a celebration. In honor of this historic event, I'm taking you and Derek out for the afternoon.''

''Sounds good,'' I said. ''Where are we going?''

''I can't tell you—it's a Mystery Ride.''

For the life of me, I couldn't imagine where Pete was taking us as we drove along in his bright green truck. He wouldn't tell us, either. So I was absolutely thrilled when the destination turned out to be Sweet Tooth.

''You remembered,'' I cried out happily. ''What a decent thing to do.'' I had told Pete the story of how I practically lusted after the Chocolate Fantasy Sundae the one time the Winners took us there and Mrs. Winner had shamed me into ordering the mini-cone.

''Go for it,'' Pete said. ''Get the works. Think of me as helping fulfill at least one of your fantasies.''

I ordered whipped cream and marshmallow plus nuts and Reese's Pieces mixed in. Pete ordered the same and little Derek pointed to the picture of the Kiddie Clown Sundae on the menu.

The waitress put our order in front of us and I sighed in pure ecstasy. No wonder they called it a Chocolate Fantasy Sundae.

''So,'' Pete said, digging his spoon into the thick hot fudge, ''what's new with you and the Bore Next Door?''

''Kindly refrain from making those snide comments about Todd Crowley,'' I said as Pete suddenly leaned forward and said, ''Look who's coming in.''

I turned around to look, expecting to see Todd Crowley, but it wasn't him. And it seemed as if everyone in the place was looking in the same direction.

There was Lisa Winner, walking through the door. She was holding hands with a guy. The two of them were all in white—white shirts, tight jeans.

They were both so beautiful they could take your breath away.

They even looked alike—the same color hair, the same flawless tan, both of them slim with such perfect features you couldn't pull your eyes off them.

''Oh, miss, may I have your autograph,'' Pete grabbed at Lisa's arm as she walked past, not even noticing us.

She turned with a start. ''Oh, Pete. And Ellen. And, oh, look—this is my little brother Derek. And this,'' she smiled radiantly, looking up at her boyfriend, ''this is Jon, without an h. Jon Harris.''

Jon lifted his sunglasses and I saw he had these incredible light gray-green eyes, one of which happened to be a black eye.''

Pete whistled. ''Wow—where'd you get that shiner?''

Lisa and Jon looked at each other. ''He had a fight with Todd Crowley,'' she whispered finally.

''No kidding.'' A big grin broke over Pete's face

and he motioned for them to sit down in our booth. "What's this? I thought Toddy was a lover, not a fighter."

"They were fighting over you, weren't they?" I blurted out, hoping the jealousy didn't show in my voice.

"Well, sort of. We were at this party and Todd called Jon a terrible name . . ."

"I'm a hairdresser," Jon said dryly. "So you can figure out what he said."

Then I realized what was different about Lisa. "It's your hair," I said. "It looks—fantastic."

Lisa's hair was done in an old-fashioned knot piled on top of her head with wispy curls and tendrils on the sides. Only Lisa could have hair that looked so perfectly tousled. Not me—mine looked like a windblown mess. I caught sight of myself in the Coca-Cola wall mirrors, and my hair looked like I'd stuck my skull in a mixer.

"Did you hear that?" Lisa asked Jon breathlessly. "She says my hair looks fantastic. Jon did my hair," she added. The two of them were practically drooling over each other.

They sat with us for a while. It was hard to hold a conversation with them. They only spoke when we asked them questions—namely questions about hairstyling. Pete and I tried to joke with them, but neither of them had a sense of humor.

We finished our sundaes. Pete, Derek and I said good-bye to them, but they hardly noticed. As Pete paid the check, I sneaked a peek back at the booth. Lisa and John were drowning in each other's eyes, not saying a word.

"Well, now we know Lisa's big secret," Pete said as we walked out to his truck.

"Who do they remind you of?" I asked Pete. "There's something familiar about Lisa and Jon—they remind me of some couple, but I can't think of who."

"How about Barbie and Ken?" Pete said, starting up the truck.

All the way back to the house, I felt like singing, that's how happy I was. Finally, Todd had realized Lisa liked somebody else. Now maybe he'd notice me.

As we pulled up in front of the house, who should be sitting on the front steps, scowling.

"Where've you been?" Marcie demanded.

I practically fell out of the truck. "What are *you* doing here? I thought you were going away for the weekend?"

"It was gross, horrible, disgusting," Marcia exploded. "We went to this dumb place for lunch with Grandma's old-lady friends. You know what they talked about?" Her voice rose. "Stool softeners, that's what. Do you know what a stool softener is?"

Pete ruffled her hair. "Hey, come on, kid. Don't be that way."

Marcie slapped at his hand. "And you should see the TV set Grandma has—it's a teeny little black-and-white. Not even color TV."

Grandma Brill came out on the porch, looking frazzled. The bright green polka-dot bow in her hair was drooping down around her ear. Her curls stuck out straight, as if she'd been running her hand through her hair. Poor Grandma—I could only imagine what a number Marcie must have done on her.

"Ellen," Grandma said, her face brightening, "when did you get back?"

''Just now.''

''Oh—because the boy next door stopped by and asked for you.''

''*Todd*?'' I looked wildly around at the Crowley's driveway. The Camaro wasn't there. ''How long ago did he stop by?''

''About ten minutes ago,'' Grandma said. ''Then I noticed him driving off somewhere.''

Could this be happening to me? Twice? That I'd missed out on a party or even a date with Todd? Maybe now that Todd had found out Lisa liked Jon, I had a chance.

But I kept missing him. Upstairs in my room, I didn't know whether to laugh or cry. All I knew was one thing:

Pete McIntyre was a regular jinx. Guys with red hair weren't just Bad News—they were Bad Luck!

17

'This is Mona Mumford,'' Grandma Brill said proudly. ''She writes beautiful poetry.''

Mona had a wide, angry face. ''Not just beautiful poetry—I also write beautiful short stories and novels, too!'' She glared at Grandma, then turned to me. ''But you'll notice all this group ever mention is my *poetry*.''

''But Mona,'' Grandma Brill said meekly, ''in all these years, we've never heard you read anything *except* your poetry. We never heard your stories and novels.''

Mona gave an angry snort and flounced over to the sofa, her brown dress hiking up over heavy, blue-veined legs. Grandma Brill took my arm and introduced me to everyone. ''This is Ellen Gardner, our mother's helper,'' she told them. ''Ellen wants to be a writer, too, so I invited her to sit in on our writers' group meeting tonight.''

In her bright yellow pantsuit and matching bow in her hair, Grandma Brill looked like a happy little yellow canary as she hopped around the living room, clutching my arm.

''. . . And this is Libby and her neighbor . . . and, oh my, I forgot your name . . . oh, that's right, Ernest, of course . . . Ernest Weems . . . Ernest is writing such a lovely . . . what? . . . oh, the coffee's in the kitchen and . . .''

Chairs had been placed to form a circle. I sat down on the one nearest to the foyer, listening to everyone talk.

I wanted to pinch myself to make sure I wasn't dreaming. Here I was—me, Ellen Gardner—with a bunch of Real Writers. I sat listening to everyone talk. They were discussing the Cape Cod Writers' Conference.

"This is something Ellen might want to know about for next summer," Libby Dwyer said, giving me a kind smile. "They have scholarships for young writers like you, Ellen."

Those words thrilled me—"young writers like you." Everyone seemed to be looking at me. I could feel myself blushing, but I was in heaven.

Ernest Weems handed me a brochure. "You can keep it," he said. "It tells you about the conference. They hold it every August right here in Craigville."

Mona was getting impatient. She wanted the meeting to start. "Let's do some writing exercises," she said in her bossy voice.

Grandma Brill had explained that the group usually did half an hour of writing exercises and that after that they read something aloud, either what they had just written or something they had done previously.

Nobody could decide what subject to write about. Mona took care of that quickly enough. "The theme of the exercise is to describe how a flower looks to a bumblebee," she announced loudly, as if daring anyone to argue with her. "Of course, you can write on another theme if you want," she added. The implication was that if you wrote about anything else you were pretty stupid, a terrible writer, or both.

Pencils and pens flew over sheets of paper as everyone started writing furiously. Except me. I kept trying to picture how a flower would look to a bumblebee, but I drew a blank. Instead, I copied from memory a poem I had written back in February when I had a terrible crush on Matt Worley at school.

"Time's up," announced one lady. She was wearing a long skirt that reached the floor. "Let's start with Walter."

Grandma had told me that the group gave constructive criticism. "We critique each other's work," she said. I sat expectantly, waiting to hear what Walter had written.

He was a youngish man with a light brown beard. He read a scene from a play he was writing. It was so confusing and so long that Mona stood up and said he should stop because there wouldn't be enough time for the others to read their work and get feedback.

Everyone seemed so relieved that Walter had stopped reading that they all gave him these flowery compliments. At least that's how I figured it.

Libby was next. Even though she had done the writing exercise, she preferred to read a poem she had written. It was nice and short and it made sense. I realized afterward that usually if the group couldn't understand something, it got a whole lot more attention.

The next person started to read a chapter of her novel. The telephone rang. Marcie had been given instructions to answer the phone in the den, where she was playing card games with Derek. A few seconds later, she poked her head into the living room. "Phone call for you," Marcie said, pointing to somebody, we weren't sure who.

"Who are you pointing at?" Grandma Brill asked.

"I forgot her name," Marcie said. "The lady with the blue veins that stick out on her legs."

"Which one?" Grandma asked, not thinking. When she realized what she had said, she clapped her hand over her mouth. "Oh, my—I didn't mean . . ."

Nobody was wearing stockings, so it actually could have been anyone. But the fact was, I knew Marcie was just being mean. She knew the woman's name. Finally, after a lot of pointing and head shaking by Marcie, the woman was identified. She had straw-colored hair and an orange dress. She stood up and asked coldly, "Where is the phone?"

What a terror Marcie was. And nobody did much to shut her up, either. Mrs. Winner ignored her, Mr. Winner was off in another galaxy, and poor Grandma couldn't do anything about her.

Somebody else started to read their work when there was the sound of a loud giggle out in the foyer. I tiptoed out of the living room to investigate. Marcie was crouched on the foor and Derek was next to her.

"You promised you'd stay in the den tonight," I whispered to Marcie. "No funny stuff now."

Marcie stood up. "There's nothing good on TV," she said in a loud whisper. "And I want to hear what Mona the Moaner is gonna read tonight. Her stuff is so goofy."

"Back to the den," I said, giving Marcie and Derek a gentle push in the right direction. I returned to my seat.

Mona was giving her opinion. "Yes, well, it does evoke a certain nuance," she was saying. "But you need more show and less tell, Wesley."

That got Mona an argument with Ernest, who thought the piece was just lovely. "The symbolism of the vampire bat was very meaningful, *I* think," he sniffed.

Then it was my turn to read. I took a deep breath. "This is something I wrote last winter," I said.

"Louder, louder," Mona said impatiently. "We can't hear you."

"My poem is called *It Is Winter*," I said loudly. I began to read:

> "It is October 13th
> And it is Winter.
>
> I feel him creeping up on me
> Putting coldness in my heart
> And ice in my soul.
>
> Yet still from far away and
> Long ago, summer breathes
> His fiery breath into me and
> Makes me live again.
>
> But only at night when I
> Dream of warm springs melting
> The ice into pools of warmth
> That make me ache
> And wish for Winter's
> Easy coolness to freeze me
> Once again."

There was a hush after I finished reading. Then Grandma Brill clapped her hands and cried, "Oh, that's beautiful."

"How old did you say you were?" Mona asked, her eyes narrowed.

Everyone praised my poem and said I had a lot of feeling and depth.

I loved it. This was praise from Real Writers! I wanted to tell them about all the other things I've written. I wished I had my notebook with me.

"We're spending too much time on that girl," Mona grumbled. "Let's move along." Actually, we hadn't spent much time on me at all. But you could tell Mona was just dying to read what she had written. She kept rattling her papers.

Finally, it was her turn. "Tonight," Mona announced, sounding quite important, "I shall read what I wrote for the exercise—about how the bumblebee felt on viewing the inside of the flower."

Mona was the only one so far who had written on that subject. There was a murmur, and everyone straightened up in their seats to hear Mona, who had marched to the middle of the living room. Everyone else had sat right where they were to read—but not Mona. Instead, she was acting out her poem with dramatic gestures and a deep stage voice.

> "Deep in the waxy, bottomless vortex—
> Muted by opiates, dulled by the hum of
>   distant beings—
> As it whirled and stretched in a caco-
>   phony of sound
> Pollinating, reverberating.
> Antennae bend in the mindless wind,
> The pollen sings a Siren song
> And the bumblebee sucks—"

Here, Mona was interrupted by a loud giggle from

the foyer. She frowned, waiting for the noise to stop. There was silence once more.

Mona resumed reading. Her arm outstretched like an orator's, Mona enunciated each word loudly and emphatically.

In her loud, carrying voice, she repeated dramatically: *"And the bumblebee sucks—"*

"AND SO DOES YOUR POEM, MONA!" cried a simpering, falsetto voice, unmistakably belonging to Marcie Winner.

Libby and her neighbor burst out laughing. Ernest Weems snickered. But Mona Mumford kept on reading her poem, trying to ignore Marcie. The more she kept reading, the more everyone seemed to have uncontrollable fits of laughing—even little Grandma Brill, who had covered her mouth.

I bit my lip trying to stop the giggles. I had to leave the meeting for a while. I went into the bathroom and splashed cold water on my face. When I came back to the living room, everyone had quieted down. They must have felt guilty, because they were all praising Mona's poem and saying how visual and meaningful it was.

But I was afraid to stay. I was worried that another fit of laughing might hit me. So instead I went into the kitchen and made another pot of coffee and rinsed off the dishes.

That night when I went to bed, I was too wound up to fall alseep. I kept remembering what Libby had said after I read my poem. "That was very honest, Ellen," she said. "It really touched me."

And as I tossed and turned, I suddenly understood what it was all about.

I sat up and snapped on the lamp. *That was it!*

That was the difference between Mona's writing

and mine. Mona had simply taken a lot of four-syllable words and strung them together like beads on a necklace, words without honesty or feeling.

But I had taken my feelings and put them into words. And I had been able to make someone think, "Ah, yes—I understand that." I had been able to touch someone's heart. And that's what a Real Writer is supposed to do.

I snapped off the lamp on the night table and turned my pillow over. The last thought before falling asleep was that someday I was going to be a Real Writer.

Me—Ellen Jane Gardner. A Real Writer.

It sounded perfectly natural!

18

"See that white house?" Marcie pointed a sticky finger. "Lisa's friend, Mandy, lives there. They caught Mandy shoplifting at Filene's."

Going for a walk with Marcie Winner was the most educational kind of house tour. She knew things about houses and their residents that amazed me.

"And this place." Marcie lowered her voice as we walked past a yellow frame house, "Some big bookie lives here. They say he bought this house through some crooked deal. I heard my mother tell someone that."

It wasn't often Marcie would go for a walk with me. I managed to drag her out by pretending we were playing Robinson Crusoe going out on an adventure. Marcie, of course, was Robinson Crusoe and Derek was playing the sidekick, Friday. "That works out good," Marcie said, "because Derek doesn't talk much either, just like Friday."

I needed to go to the drugstore. We had been playing Careers when I realized why I'd been feeling blah and droopy for the past couple of days. Also why a big zit had blossomed on my chin. It was, as they say in the ads, that certain time of the month coming up. I needed to get some maxi-pads.

As we crossed the street, a garbage truck was loading up noisily. The garbage men were a jolly bunch, laughing loudly and yelling to each other. One of them seemed a lot younger, probably summer help. He was wearing a baseball cap turned backwards. He looked about 18 or 19, not much more.

"Hey, there—you in the yellow blouse," he called out to me, "where've you *been* all my life?"

"Under a garbage can!" Marcie shot back before I could even answer.

He shrugged. Whistling loudly, he picked up some trash bags from the curb. Then, with a noisy stripping of gears, the garbage truck lumbered off and around the corner.

What a letdown. I mean, just when some guy was flirting with me and giving me an ego boost, wouldn't you know Marcie would ruin it. "Why," I asked, "did you have to say *that*?"

Marcie looked at me surprised. "Listen—if that's the best you can do, you better hang it up. When *I'm* fifteen," she added, "I'll do a lot better than hanging out with garbage boys."

I stopped in the middle of the sidewalk. "You know something, Marcie—that book in the library was *right* about you. I looked up the meaning of your name. And you know what 'Marcella' means? It means '*warlike*'. That's right—your name comes from Mars, the god of war. So how do you like *that*?"

As it turned out, Marcie did, in fact, like that. "Warlike," she repeated proudly. "I'm named for the god of war. Hey, Derek, I wonder what 'Ellen' means. She's probably named after the god of wimps." With that, Marcie covered her mouth in a fit of giggles.

I didn't bother to answer. Derek walked between the two of us, skipping and smiling. He loved being outdoors. Marcie pointed out a couple of other landmarks and before we knew it, we were at Jensen's Drugstore.

I'd never seen a drugstore like it. It was all done in this old-fashioned style, with Tiffany lamps, antique-looking mirrors, and velvety carpeting, except around the soda fountain.

The place was crowded. Tourists were there buying postcards—ladies in expensive-looking shifts, girls with freshly shampooed hair, and barefoot kids with T-shirts and cutoff jeans. They all looked tan and healthy.

It took me a while to find what I needed. They had this cutesy way of hiding "Personal Needs" products. Finally, I had to ask the pharmacist where they were. With my luck, naturally, he was old and hard-of-hearing.

"Oh," Marcie said. "That's why you wanted to go for a walk. You needed some Mickey Mouse Mattresses."

"We don't carry Mickey Mouse watches," the deaf old pharmacist scowled. "Only Timex."

"No, no," I said louder, feeling my face turn red. "I'm looking for—uh—maxi-pads."

"Then why'd you ask about wristwatches?" he grumbled.

Marcie and Derek went over to the soda fountain to get ice cream cones while I stood in line, waiting to pay the cashier. Just as I was handing over the money, Derek came over. His mouth was already smeared with fudge ripple. He pointed to the box I was handing the cashier.

"Maxi-pads," Derek shrilled. Everyone stared at us. "Maxi-pads," he repeated.

The one thing Derek finally said clearly, and it had to be something that made me cringe! I felt so embarrassed. A lady in back of me tapped my shoulder and whispered, "You shouldn't teach your brother such things. It's not nice." Marcie had sidled over, giving me sly looks and giggling. I knew she had coached Derek.

The cashier handed me my purchase in a bag and I grabbed Derek's hand, hurrying him outside.

"That was a sleezy thing to do," I told her when we were on the street. "Stop teaching that stuff to Derek."

We walked back in silence. Streams of melting ice cream dripped down Derek's cone. Marcie grabbed it, licked around the cone, and before Derek even realized what was happening, she had finished the entire thing.

"I shouldn't have come," she complained. "Look how hot it is. And there was a good movie on, too—about this monster who'd buried in ice—" She broke off suddenly and snickered, "Speaking of monsters, look over there."

I looked—and my heart started beating faster. There, across the street, was a sight more thrilling than a sunset: Todd Crowley in jogging shorts.

He had a white sweatband on his forehead and his rippling muscles glistened with sweat. It looked like he worked out, but he must have concentrated on his chest and arms, because his legs were really thin.

Marcie noticed that too. "Hey, clod," she said as he came closer to us, "how come you got those big bulgy muscles on top but your legs are like sticks? It looks like you'll tip over one of these days."

"When are they going to put a lid on you?" Todd said, shaking his head. The two of them started in on each other. "How come you're wearing that handkerchief on your forehead?" Marcie said. "It looks like you got wounded in the brain.''

''Maybe I should put this over your mouth,'' Todd said, pulling off the sweatband and winking at me.

I tried to change the subject. ''So—you're jogging, huh?'' I said to Todd.

''No, stupid—he's chopping wood,'' Marcie snapped before Todd could answer. ''What do you think he's doing in that outfit?''

''What are *you* doing in that outfit?'' Todd gestured at Marcie's gray jogging suit. ''You ought to try jogging off some of those pounds.''

Marcie didn't answer. She shot Todd an angry look and grabbed Derek's hand. ''Come on—let's go home.''

Todd fell into step beside me. I noticed he had a bandage on his chin. I wondered if it was a souvenir from his fistfight with Lisa's boyfriend, Jon.

''Looks like you bought out the store,'' Todd said, looking down at the big paper bag I was carrying with the economy-size box of maxi-pads inside. ''Want me to carry that for you?''

''No, no,'' I said hastily. Behind me, I heard Marcie snicker.

''Well, cutekins,'' Todd gave me that dazzling smile of his, ''how goes the battle?''

''I don't think I'm winning,'' I said. Just then Marcie tugged at my paper bag. ''Derek wants to carry that,'' she said. ''He needs to wipe his hands on the bag—they're all sticky.''

''The bag is bigger than Derek,'' I said. ''It's too heavy for him.''

''No it's not. I'll help him carry it.''

''Oh, all right.'' I really didn't want to hand the bag to Marcie, but I wanted her to stop bugging me so I could concentrate on talking to Todd.

Behind us, Marcie and Derek kept whispering and giggling. I was glad they were busy so they wouldn't bother me.

We were almost home. "I've got to get some more running time in," Todd said. "Another fifteen minutes or so. Good seeing you."

Off he jogged. I watched him, my heart twisting. He was so gorgeous—everything I wanted in a guy.

I could hear the faint sound of a bag ripping and I was about to tell Derek to be careful how he was wiping his hands. But I was practically hypnotized watching Todd as he disappeared down the street.

Pete's truck was parked in the driveway. Out of the corner of my eye, I noticed Pete walking down the front stairs.

"Yo, Ellen," he called out. "Did Mrs. Winner leave my check anywhere? Grandma Brill doesn't know where it is."

I was just about to answer when there was a smothered giggle and Marcie's laugh rang out. Derek was giggling too. I whirled around, and what I saw made me want to die, right there on the sidewalk.

Derek had one maxi-pad taped around his forehead like Todd's sweatband.

Another maxi-pad was taped around his mouth like he was a doctor with a surgical mask.

The box was on the sidewalk, big as life. Three of four pads were falling out where the box was ripped open.

A red-hot wave of humiliation shot through me.

"Oh, goodness me, look what silly little Derek did," Marcie said innocently. "Silly, silly, Derek."

"Maxi-pads," Derek said clear as can be.

I wanted the sidewalk to rise up and cover me. Marcie's beady little eyes darted from me to Pete.

"Goodness gracious," she simpered, "just look what Derek did to Ellen's package over there."

Like, just in case Pete couldn't figure out who the maxi-pads belonged to.

Pete surprised me. He handled it all with class. "Look, you two—knock it off," he said sharply. He took the pads from Derek and put them into what was left of the paper bag. "And pick those up *now*. They cost money."

He gathered up the box and carried it into the house. "And if I ever catch you pulling anything like that again, I'll break your head," he told Marcie.

My face was scorching. "Don't be embarrassed, Ellen," Pete said calmly. "I've got sisters. In my house, they buy these things by the carload."

I snatched the box from Pete's hands and raced upstairs. In the bathroom, I realized I had bought the maxi-pads just in time.

Later on as I was setting the table for dinner, Marcie mumbled, "We were only kidding. You didn't have to be such a baby about it."

I didn't say a word. I gave her the silent treatment, which drives her crazy. And I refused to tell her the ending of a story I had made up about a kid who turned into a werewolf.

My only consolation was that at least it had happened in front of Pete. Because if the incident had happened in front of Todd Crowley, Marcie Winner might have been history!

19

"I'm sick and tired of being kicked around!" Marcie yelled.

"But it's just for one night, that's all," Lisa pleaded.

Mrs. Winner sat at the kitchen table, frowning over her cup of coffee as she listened to the plaintiff and defendant. Lisa was having a sleep-over party that night and wanted Marcie out of the bedroom.

"Why *can't* I stay in the room?" Marcie demanded. "I won't bother your dumb friends."

"Oh, no, Mother," Lisa wailed, "if Marcie stays in the room, none of the girls will come. The last time I had a sleep-over, Marcie hung around and listened to everything we talked about. Then she blabbed it all over school and it ruined Pam's reputation."

"I only told Bobby Brain," Marcie said. "He promised he wouldn't tell anybody else."

Mrs. Winner and Marcie held important negotiations and finally came to an agreement. Marcie would sleep downstairs on the sofa in the den. In return, Mr. and Mrs. Winner would take her out to dinner Sunday night.

"And not one of those cheap-o places either," Marcie said. "I wanna go to a real nice, expensive restaurant like Steak-Out."

As soon as Marcie said the word "expensive", Mrs. Winner's face contorted in pain. "Oh, very well, Marcella," she said with a sigh. "But you have to promise you won't bother your sister and her friends tonight.''

I noticed that when it came to anything for Lisa, Mrs. Winner didn't complain too much. Not even when we went to the supermarket and Lisa piled chips, candy, ice cream, and soda galore into the shopping basket. Usually Mrs. Winner makes remarks about how expensive food is, but for Lisa, she was Lady Bountiful.

It was an overcast, dreary kind of Saturday. By late afternoon, my mood matched the weather. I felt like doing something creative. Grandma Brill was going out to a potluck dinner, Mr. and Mrs. Winner weren't eating at home, and Lisa was going to order pizza for her friends.

So I decided to make poor folks' pie for dinner that night. It's one of those dump-everything-all-together recipes Mom taught me to make. It's real easy—all you need is hamburger, mashed potatoes, corn, catsup, and cheese. It tastes better than it sounds.

At first Marcie didn't even want to taste it. She kept insisting on hot dogs and beans. But wonder of wonders, she actually liked it. She kept saying ''Yecch-h'' while I was fixing it, but she sure changed her tune fast once she tried it.

She and Derek were on second helping when there was a knock at the back door. It was Todd, a red windbreaker covering his head in the early-evening drizzle.

He pinched my cheek as I let him in the door. I never knew a pinch on the cheek could make me feel so happy.

''M-mmmm-mmm,'' he sniffed. ''Something smells good. What is it?''

"Ellen made poor folks pie," Marcie said. "We're playing Poverty."

"Poverty, huh? Sounds like fun." Todd caught my eye and smiled. "How do you play it?"

"See," Marcie explained, "we're making believe it's a rainy, miserable night and our roof is leaking. We're huddled together eating our pitiful meal of poor folks' pie."

Todd reached over and took a piece from my plate. "Hey," he said, swallowing a bite, "you poor folks eat pretty good."

"Well, us low-income folks know those little tricks to make food tasty."

Todd finished the rest of the piece he had taken. "I like the domestic type," he said. "The way to my heart is through my stomach."

"It sure isn't through your brain," Marcie snickered.

Todd had leaned back in the chair and was staring at me. "Something's different about you. What is it?"

"Lisa cut my hair." I was ecstatic that Todd had noticed.

"Speaking of Lisa—where is she anyhow?" Todd tried to sound casual, but he didn't fool me. My heart dropped.

"Lisa is straightening out her sty," Marcie said as she cut another big wedge of pie. "Her goony girlfriends are sleeping over tonight."

"Oh," said Todd, "a hen party." He was silent for a few minutes, thinking. "I wondered if she was going to Kevin Riddock's party," he said lamely. "I figured I could give her a ride."

Marcie gave a delicate burp. "Why don't you just hang it up?" she said. "I heard Brandy saying Lisa has a secret boyfriend. How come you're still hanging around here bugging her? She's not interested in you, Toady."

I had been rinsing off the dishes while the two of them were going back and forth, so I didn't see the expression on Todd's face when he said the Magic Words.

"Maybe the reason I hang around here is on account of your cute little mother's helper. Right, Ellen?"

I whirled around and stared at him. Todd was straddling the chair, smiling that velvet smile of his. "I bet Ellen wouldn't treat me like Lisa does if I asked her out—would you, Ellen?"

"WHEN?" I practically screamed the word out. Todd hadn't exactly asked me for a date, but it was close enough. "When did you want to go out?"

A grin broke over his face. "Well, I didn't exactly mean—well, hey, why not? Okay, let's see. I'm going to Maine for a few days. I'll be back next Thursday. How about then?"

"No—not Thursday," I suddenly felt very assertive. "I want to go out Saturday. I'm a Saturday night girl."

"A Saturday night girl," Todd repeated. "I like that. All right then—next Saturday, a week from tonight."

Marcie, who had been listening to the whole thing with her mouth hanging open, made a rude noise. "Yuck—who'd want to go out with Toad Crawley? You mean it's *Toad* you like?" she said to me. "Wow—you need a brain transplant."

Todd ignored her. He stood up, kissed the top of my head, and said softly, "Okay, cute stuff. Save yourself for me."

I could feel myself melting like butter in a microwave.

As usual, Marcie was ruining the mood. "You don't fool me, Toad," she yelled after him. "You're trying to make Lisa jealous by asking Ellen out. Only Lisa doesn't care."

Marcie sat back down on her chair and added slyly, "I know who *does* care, though—Brandy Simms!"

In fact, just to make sure Brandy knew that Todd was taking me out next Saturday, Marcie told her all about it the moment Brandy and the other girls walked in the house.

"Toddy is *so* democratic," Brandy drawled. "He always *did* mingle with the hired help." Everybody laughed. I felt like slapping her.

For the next couple of hours, Brandy did her best to make me feel like hired help. She kept calling downstairs from Lisa's phone, asking for more ice or another bag of potato chips. Luckily, Derek loves to run errands, so he brought everything up to Lisa's room.

Meanwhile, back in the den, I was playing rummy with Marcie and watching an old movie on TV. I was trying to pretend I was enjoying myself. Lisa and her friends upstairs were dancing and laughing so loud I couldn't concentrate. I felt kind of lonely. *It isn't easy being a mother's helper*, I thought to myself. Especially at the Winner house. And especially when I compared myself with Lisa and Brandy and Candy and Mandy. They had all the fun and I felt weighted down with responsibilities.

It just wasn't fair.

Around 9 o'clock it got quiet upstairs. The phone rang. "Oh, Ellen," Lisa asked in her breathless voice, "would you mind coming up here. I'm giving Candy a haircut and I want to show her how I cut yours."

"All right," I said, not very enthusiastically. I didn't feel like seeing Lisa's friends. But Marcie was only too happy to accompany me upstairs and see what was going on. Derek followed us.

Lisa's bedroom looked like a relief center after a major earthquake. There were sleeping bags and clothes strewn all around, plus cans of Coca-Cola, candy wrappers, and potato chip crumbs. Marcie was furious. She kept yelling about getting roaches.

Candy was sitting at Lisa's dressing table, her hair wet. Lisa scrunched up a section of Candy's light brown hair. "I thought I'd cut yours short on the sides like I did with Ellen."

Candy looked at me and nodded. "Okay. I like Ellen's haircut."

It was like getting the Good Housekeeping Seal of Approval.

I sat down on the carpet next to Marcie and Derek, watching as Lisa started to cut Candy's hair. Some other girls whose names I didn't know, because nobody had introduced us, were laughing and talking about boys and parties.

"I don't know if *I'd* like your hair cut that way," Brandy said. "It's all right for Ellen, but . . ." She made a face. It was as if she were telling them: *That haircut is all right for the hired help—but not for our crowd.*

We heard the sound of a key in the downstairs back door. Grandma Brill was home from her potluck dinner and bingo game.

"Hello?" she called out. "Hello? Where are you? Who's upstairs?"

"Burglars, lady," Marcie shouted back.

Brandy let out a whoop. "I just love it. This family is too much."

Grandma Brill was sighing her way up the stairs. She crept into Lisa's room, holding the side of her face. "Another tooth," she moaned. "I was eating tuna casserole and my back tooth crumbled. See?" She lifted a folded handkerchief and showed us a tiny piece of something grayish white.

"Oh, gross," Marcie said.

But Lisa went over and hugged Grandma. "I'm so sorry," she said in her sweet voice. "I'm so sorry about your tooth, Grandma."

"Well what do you expect?" Marcie said, her mouth full of potato chips from an extra bag she had retrieved. "You're an old lady, Grandma. Your teeth are supposed to be falling out."

Brandy and the other girls were laughing. Poor Grandma was practically in tears. "But it's not like I was chewing–tuna casserole isn't hard–it just crumbled, just like *that*."

"That's what happens," Marcie said philosophically. "You get old, you get brown spots on your hands, and varicose veins and quivery arms, and your teeth crumble out of your head."

Brandy was laughing that loud, horsey laugh of hers. I thought she'd fall off the bed. "Oh, I just love it when Marcie and your grandmother go at it," she gasped.

Marcie glared at Brandy. "Don't you make fun of my grandma," she warned.

Brandy laughed louder than ever. "Oh, that's rich. Bratkins is upset because she thinks I'm laughing at her grandma. Do you believe it?"

With that, she threw her head back and laughed

so hard that she knocked the towel from Candy's shoulders. Little wisps of light brown hair were strewn all over the blue carpet.

"Oh, dear, look at that mess," Brandy declared, kicking the tufts of hair with her bare foot. "Ellen, get the vacuum and clean this up now or we'll get hair all over us when we do our yoga."

At first I thought she was joking. But then she flashed me a mocking look and I knew she must have knocked over the towel on purpose.

Everybody was looking at me expectantly. I was so upset I couldn't speak.

"Unless I am mistaken," Brandy said with a haughty lift of her blond head, "I do believe Ellen is the mother's helper around here."

Lisa said hesitantly, "Ellen, would you please get the vacuum out?"

Not in a million years, I thought. *Even if it means getting fired on the spot and going back to Pawtucket. Even if it means never going out with Todd.* "I'm off duty," I said, pulling myself up from the carpet.

"I'll get the vacuum," Grandma started to say. She was always the peacemaker.

"Oh, no! That's Ellen's job," Brandy said. She stood there, looking tall and rich and mean.

It was a scene I'll never forget. Lisa stood there, scissors frozen in midair over Candy's head. Grandma was blinking, Derek was blowing tufts of hair around the carpet, and everybody was silently watching.

Marcie's voice shattered the calm. "Don't you *ever, ever* tell Ellen what to do!" she exploded. "SHE'S NOT *YOUR* MOTHER'S HELPER–SHE'S *MY* MOTHER'S HELPER!"

In a daze, I followed Marcie and Derek downstairs to the den. The three of us sat in front of the TV, but for the life of me, I still can't remember what we watched.

A few minutes later, we heard the whir of the vacuum cleaner upstairs in Lisa's bedroom. Marcie didn't say a word about it. Neither did I.

I never did find out who vacuumed the hair off the carpet.

All I know is, it wasn't me!

20

From the moment I woke up the next morning, all I could think about was my date with Todd. *One week from tonight*, I thought to myself ecstatically.

I planned out every detail so I would look my very best—which day to give myself an Apricot Facial Scrub . . . when to do my nails . . . what I should wear. I kept wishing I had something really great-looking, but the only decent outfit I had was a pair of white slacks Mom had bought me before I left Pawtucket.

Now, let's see, I thought to myself, *with my white sandals, and my new lucky earrings, and a good tan . . .*

The trouble was, my tan was fading. Just to be spiteful, Marcie managed to keep me inside the house during Prime Tanning Time. And I really needed to work on my tan so I could look good for Todd. I did have a plan in the works along those lines, but it depended on Bobbie-Lou and I was afraid it might not happen in time.

I tried to make the best of the long, draggy weekend. On Saturday night, we all went out food shopping. On Sunday, we went to a flea market. The less said about Sundays with Mr. and Mrs. Winner, the better.

On Monday, I thought up a way to get Marcie outside.

"We're playing Lifeboat," I explained. "Make believe we were in a shipwreck and now we're the only survivors in this teensy little lifeboat in the middle of the Pacific Ocean. The hot, tropical sun is beating down brutally on us." As I spoke, I turned my lounge chair to face the sun.

"No fair!" Marcie cried. "You're trying to sneak in a tan."

"No I'm not. I'm just facing this way so I can see if there's any ships coming to rescue us."

"I don't like this game." Marcie wiped beads of sweat from her forehead. "And how come we gotta eat tuna fish for lunch?"

"Oh, be realistic," I told her. "People in the middle of the ocean wouldn't have anything else to eat except fish. And I mean *real* fish—not sardines." That shut Marcie up.

Derek, at least, liked the game. Marcie decided he could be the native guide who was supposed to fan us. He kept going from Marcie to me, fanning us with his book of nursery rhymes.

I managed to stay outside for one hour and 10 minutes. I got some good color on my face, too.

On Tuesday morning, Julienne and Nedra came over to do the weekly cleaning.

I could never get used to seeing Julienne, all dressed up in a sharp-looking outfit with her good jewelry, getting out of her Mercedes, and then changing into old clothes to clean the Winner house.

I was busy, as usual, in the laundry room. "Girl, you are sure getting real good with that iron," Nedra joked. She sat down and talked with me for a while about the clothes she was buying for college and what subjects she was planning to take. After being ignored and put down by Lisa's friends, it felt good to have someone bright and pretty like Nedra to talk to.

Right before lunch, Lisa came home. She had been staying overnight in Boston at Brandy's aunt's condominium. Lisa must have gone on a shopping safari, because she was loaded down with boxes and packages.

Julienne, Nedra and Grandma Brill took a break from cleaning to see what Lisa had bought. I shut off the iron and followed them into the living room.

''I just *love* those Boston stores,'' Lisa told us, holding up a white-and-black shopping bag that read ''BADD'S GOODS''. ''Don't you just *love* this name? And look—they give you a free bumper sticker, too. Look what it says—'I'M A *BADD* GIRL.' Get it? Isn't that darling?'' Lisa seemed to like the shopping bag and bumper sticker from the store a lot better than the sweater she had bought there.

''OOOH-WEE,'' Julienne said straight-faced. ''Miz Lisa, you sure are one smart shopper. Look at that—she got a *free* bumper sticker. Me oh my.''

Lisa took that as a compliment. ''Oh, thank you, Julienne,'' she said very seriously.

We were so busy ooh-ing and aah-ing over Lisa's purchases that we didn't notice Marcie and Derek come into the room.

''More clothes?'' Marcie shook her head in disgust as she looked at the clothes and packages Lisa had strewn all over the living room sofa. ''You don't *need* any more clothes. You've got things you've never worn. You just like to get those shopping bags and bumper stickers, that's all.''

Nothing seemed to bother Lisa. She just smiled her vague little smile and pulled the string off a shoe box. "And look." She held up a pair of white leather pumps. "They have this adorable store called Shoe 'Nuff. Isn't that name precious?"

"Just darling," Marcie said, imitating Lisa's breathless little voice. "But how come such a precious, adorable shoe store didn't even give you one of their cute little shopping bags? All you got was a shoe box."

"That's right." Lisa looked crushed. "And I bet they had a cute shopping bag, too."

Marcie rolled her eyes. "See what I mean?" She asked, looking around at everyone. "Lisa just doesn't connect."

Julienne was peering at the price tag on a pair of jeans. "Oh, girl," she wagged a finger at Lisa, "you better marry someone rich, 'cause you got expensive taste."

Grandma Brill and Derek helped Lisa carry the packages upstairs. Marcie watched them, looking like she was about to cry.

"It's not fair," she said. "Everyone spoils Lisa rotten. She gets everything she wants. But nobody cares about me and Derek."

"Now, honey," Julienne started to say, but Marcie didn't let her finish.

"Julienne, you *know* it's true. Lisa gets all the attention. She's the only one they wanted. Well, maybe they like Derek because he's the baby and he's cute. But they don't care about *me*!"

"Why do you say that?" Nedra asked.

"Because it's true." Marcie stood there, in her yellow-and-black jogging suit, looking like an angry bumblebee. "You know what my mother called me and Derek? She called us The Afterthoughts." Marcie was so upset that she could barely talk. "She was joking about it one time when they had some people over. I heard my mother say she was so busy with some big estate case she didn't even know she was going to have me!"

"Marcie, honey, your momma has a big career and all," Julienne said lamely.

"When Lisa was a baby, they used to take her everywhere," Marcie went on. "You told me that. Pete said so, too. They brought her to the office and let her play all day. They never took me and Derek there. They never took us anywhere."

"That's 'cause your folks got to be real big lawyers," Jullienne said. "They could afford to have someone take care of you."

"Oh, sure, my mother's always *paying* someone to stay with us." Marcie sounded bitter. "Either it's a housekeeper or a maid or a dopey mother's helper every summer."

Nedra and I stole glances at each other. It was as if Marcie and Julienne didn't even know we were there.

"My mother doesn't *have* to go to the office every single day," Marcie kept on. "And she and Father are always out at night. Why can't she stay home sometimes and take care of us?"

Julienne put her big hand on Marcie's shoulder. "Sugar, your folks care about you," she said. Marcie didn't answer. She turned abruptly and went into the den. We could hear the sound of the channel switcher clicking away.

"What you two starin' at?" Julienne turned to us angrily. "Nedra, you finish that dusting, hear? And you, Ellen—you got plenty of ironing back there. Now scoot!"

We scooted. From the laundry room, I could hear

Julienne grumbling as she talked to herself. "No decorum around this house," she kept saying.

Right after lunch, the mail came. Grandma Brill always said you could almost set your watch by the mailman. That was what I'd been banking on in my Tan Plan, if it ever came to pass. Leafing through the pile of mail, Grandma Brill said in surprise, "Oh, Marcie, here's something for you."

"For me?" Marcie's mood perked up. So did mine. "I bet this is from Bobby Brain," she said, taking a white envelope from Grandma. "He said he was going to visit his father after camp was over." She tore open the envelope and read what was inside.

And then she sat down again at the table and reread the slip of paper.

"I don't get it," she said, frowning. "Somebody sent me a chain letter."

"A chain letter? Really?" My voice had the proper tone of surprise. "Let me see what it says."

The letter read:

Dear Marcie,

This is a Chain Letter. It has been sent to many people all over the world & they have all received Good Luck from it!!! IF YOU BREAK THIS CHAIN, YOU WILL HAVE *VERY BAD LUCK!!!*

Keep up the GOOD LUCK & avoid the EVIL CURSE by sending this letter plus a copy of the Good Luck Prayer also enclosed to *TEN OTHER PEOPLE!* Write these letters the same time each day. Do not let them know it was you that sent it. REMEMBER, IF YOU BREAK THIS CHAIN, YOU WILL HAVE BAD LUCK.

Signed: A Friend

P.S. Do not tell your parents about this or you will break the chain.

I put down the letter and shook my head. "Well, I guess you better start sending those letters out right away," I said. "And you have to copy the Good Luck Prayer, too."

"That prayer is awfully long," Marcie complained. "I don't write too fast. It'll take me a long time."

"You better start doing it right away," I warned her. "I know somebody who waited too long and they broke the chain and . . ."

"And what?"

"I'd rather not say." I pretended to shudder.

"Okay, okay," Marcie said hastily. "I'll start tomorrow."

"No," I cried, adding quickly, "that's not the way you're supposed to do it. You have to write one letter and one prayer the same time every day—right about now in fact."

"I don't have any stamps."

"I've got a whole book of them," I said. "But you have to write those letters outdoors."

Marcie gave me a suspicious look. "It doesn't say that."

"Huh," I told her, "maybe it doesn't exactly *say* so, but I happen to know it's extra good luck if you write a chain letter outdoors. Especially on a nice day."

"It's so hot," Marcie grumbled. "And the sun gets in my eyes."

"Oh, you can sit in the shade," I said. "Derek and I will keep you company outside."

"This is dumb," Marcie grumbled. I gave her

some of my stationery and envelopes and a purple pen. She and Derek followed me outside.

What a heavenly day. I lay down on the lounge and smeared Bain de Soleil on my nose. It was so relaxing to lie there, soaking up sun and listening to Marcie talking out loud as she slowly copied the letter and prayer.

"Suppose it rains?" she asked. "Then what?"

"Then you can write the letters inside. But only if it's raining."

"Okay, let's see," she said to herself. "I could send one to Hillary and one to Courtney and one to my grandmother Winner and one to Julienne and one to Lucy Bowels—that's five."

"How about your friend Bobby Brain?"

"Bobby's probably the one who sent me that letter in the first place," Marcie giggled. She sat up. "Hey—where's the envelope it came in?"

"Uh—I think Grandma Brill threw the envelope out," I lied. "It's in the garbage with those chicken gizzards."

"Oh, vomit," Marcie said. "Never mind. I don't wanna stick my hand into those gizzards."

"You're right," I agreed. "The letter was probably from Bobby." I didn't want Marcie to see the North Carolina postmark.

The way I figured it, this was really just a white lie. And white lies don't really count—not when you need to get a really good tan.

21

Wednesday nite

Dear Bobbie-Lou,

You wonderful, marvelous friend. THANK YOU, THANK YOU. The letter came yesterday & the timing was perfect. I need to work on my tan because BIG NEWS—I HAVE A DATE THIS SAT NITE WITH TODD!!!

Today my Mom came down—she took a vacation day. Luckily it was cloudy—good day for shopping. When she heard I had a date, she insisted on buying me a dress (twist my arm, Mom). They had a sale at Jordan Marsh. I felt guilty about her spending money on a dress but she said she's hardly had to spend money on food since I've been gone. We had a great time.

Mom met Marcie (of course, Le Brat was on good behavior—Mom thought she was a little angel). She thought Derek was darling and she also met Pete—she liked him, too (he's the kind of guy mothers like).

Oh, have to tell you this—Mom said something like, ''That blond boy who does the yard work is very nice.'' And I said to her, ''Pete's not blond, he's got red hair.''

And Mom said he didn't have red hair, he

has blond hair. She says that color hair is what they call strawberry blond. All this time, I thought Pete had red hair. When we got home from shopping, I was going to check out his hair color if he was around, but I heard he went off on a camping trip for a few days.

Oh, well—I'm not interested in Pete except as a friend. (But I'm sure interested in Todd!) Wish me luck—write soon.

Your grateful friend,
Ellen

P.S. Sorry this letter sounds so ME-ME-ME. I want to hear about YOU-YOU-YOU. Regards to your cousins.

Wed. nite

Dear Mom,

It was great seeing you & thanks for the dress—love it! I don't know what I'd have worn Sat. nite if you hadn't bought it.

I knew I forgot to tell you a funny story. Remember the black lady in the silver Mercedes who tooted at us near the mall? That was Julienne, Mrs. Winner's *cleaning lady*!!!

Pete told me Julienne is rich. Her husband won the lottery a few years ago & Mrs. W invested the money for them & made a bundle. But she still pays Julienne to clean her house every week like she always did & Julienne is afraid if she doesn't stay on as a cleaning lady, Mrs. W won't keep her on as a client. Isn't that wild? Leave it to Mrs. Winner to have the richest cleaning lady in America!

Love & XXX,
Ellen

P.S. Just want to tell you—I'm glad *you're* my mom. Love ya.

22

I don't know if a fifteen-year-old girl can actually have a heart attack, but on Friday afternoon, I thought for sure I was going to be a statistic.

I had just spotted Todd for the first time since he'd gotten back from Maine. He was washing his Camaro in the driveway, so I ran over to ask him what time he'd be coming by for me Saturday night.

He just stared at me blankly. ''Saturday night? What's happening Saturday night?''

''You didn't forget, did you?'' I stammered. There was a roaring in my ears and my chest felt like it was tied up in hundreds of little knots. ''We're supposed to go out tomorrow night—remember?'' I waited for his answer and the roaring in my ears was louder than thunder.

''Oh, yeah. Right. The Saturday night girl. That's right.'' Todd put down his polishing cloth and thought a moment. ''Let's see. Uh—figure about quarter of six, then. Okay?''

Was that *okay*? It was wonderful. It was marvelous.

It was also, according to Marcie, a strange time to be going out on a date. But Grandma Brill said that Todd must be taking me out to dinner. ''Why else would you be going out at that time?'' she reasoned.

"Todd Tightwad?" Marcie scoffed. "His Royal Cheapness wouldn't buy *anyone* dinner."

I didn't think Saturday night would ever come, but somehow it did. I took my time getting ready, fussing with my hair and doing my eyes very carefully. I was giving my teeth a final flossing when Marcie came into the room and sprawled on the bed, watching me.

She sat there, picking at her mosquito bites until they bled.

"Pick me a winner," I said. "Kindly stop picking your scabs while I'm flossing. It makes me barf."

"Speaking of barf, here's your Big Date now," Marcie commented as the doorbell rang. She raced downstairs to open the front door.

I took a quick last look in the mirror. My new aqua dress was fine, the turquoise-and-silver good luck earrings looked great with my tan, and I didn't even smudge my mascara. Even my hair came out good. I had to admit I looked nice.

Ellen came down the staircase slowly, the skirt of her aqua dress swirling gracefully. Todd stared up at her, his eyes shining. "Ellen," he whispered, "you look so very lovely. Let's—"

"Let's *go*, let's *go*!" Todd was looking at his watch. He gave me a hurried glance as I came down the stairs, then grabbed my wrist. "Come on—let's move it," he said.

I wished he had told me I looked nice, but I figured he was in a big hurry. He probably had reservations at some nice restaurant.

"I won't keep her out late," he called to Grandma Brill over his shoulder as he steered me to his car.

As we drove along, my stomach started to rumble. It was embarrassing. I had hardly eaten all week because I wanted to look nice and thin for tonight. I had skipped lunch and all I'd eaten at breakfast was a banana because it has potassium.

I hoped I wouldn't make a pig of myself when we got to the restaurant.

"This traffic is for the birds," Todd commented as he drove along. Luckily he didn't seem to notice the gurgling noises my stomach was making because he was driving so fast and looking at his watch every few minutes. Suddenly he made a right turn into the parking lot of a shopping center.

"Just in time," he said, driving to the very end of the lot and parking away from the other cars. He certainly was proud of his Camaro. I couldn't blame him. It was in beautiful condition.

"It burns me up to pay full price after six o'clock," Todd said.

"I know what you mean," I agreed. This was probably one of those restaurants that raised prices after six. Mom and I usually try to time it so we can get the early-bird dinner specials at restaurants.

I was stunned when I realized where Todd was heading. Not to a restaurant, but to the box office of the Seaview Cinema Five Theater.

"I missed this film first time around," he said. "We just made it—the prices go up after six o'clock." He bought the tickets and ushered me inside quickly, past the refreshment stand. He didn't ask if I wanted any popcorn or candy and I would never have suggested it. But oh, that popcorn smelled great. I was starving.

The only thing good I can say about the movie was that you couldn't hear my stomach making noises.

That was because it was one of those dumb horror movies where everyone is always screaming. It had to be one of the worst movies ever. I remember when that film came out—it got the most terrible review in the Pawtucket newspaper. They wouldn't even give it one star.

By the time the movie ended, I had a terrible headache. Not only because it was so loud and dumb, but because I was still so hungry. Back in Todd's car, my stomach gave a rumble that sounded like a 21-gun salute. This time Todd heard it. He said with a laugh, "I get the hint—let's grab a bite."

As we drove along, the subject of our conversation was Lisa. "So what did Lisa say when she heard I was taking you out tonight?" Todd wanted to know. He seemed disappointed when I told him Lisa hadn't said anything at all.

"That Lisa," he said, rolling her name around as if he were licking his lips. "She really gets to a guy. It's those eyes of hers. Lisa," he brooded, "has *knowing eyes*. You know what I mean?"

Knowing eyes? Lisa herself didn't know much—let alone her eyes! But, of course, I didn't say anything. I didn't want to sound jealous.

Todd took me to Hamburger Galaxy. It wasn't the romantic restaurant I'd pictured, but by then I was so hungry I didn't care. Todd had two hamburgers with everything and an order of french fries and onion rings.

All I ordered was the Venus burger, which was a fancy name for hamburger with lettuce and tomato. I didn't want Todd to think I ate a lot. And I didn't want any onion rings because I was afraid he might not want to kiss me.

It was still early when we finished. "Let's go for

a ride,'' Todd suggested. He had stopped talking about Lisa now and was getting real affectionate. ''You look so fine,'' he whispered into my ear when he stopped at a traffic light. I thought I would dissolve into little pieces.

I didn't even realize where Todd was going until he slowed down and parked the car.

We were in Passion Alley. The local make-out place.

I remembered the time Pete had pointed it out to me on the way home from Craigville Beach. Everyone joked about the place—they called it Virgin Vistas, Fantasy Island, Horny Acres, and a few other choice names.

Suddenly I felt nervous.

''Hey, hey, relax,'' Todd said with a little laugh. ''We need some mood music. Personally dedicated to you.'' He shut off the radio and put his arm around me.

''I'm gonna serenade you,'' he said, and started to sing in a low, quivery voice:

> ''Oh, you're good lookin' but you're
> gonna die someday . . .''

As he sang, his hand traced circles on my shoulder. He kept on singing:

> ''. . . Yes, you're good lookin' but you're
> gonna die someday—
> I just want some loving before you pass
> away!''

Todd pulled me over to him roughly. ''Come on now—I thought chicks from Rhode Island were friendlier than that,'' he whispered. ''I know something that'll relax you.''

With that, he opened the glove compartment and took out a leather-covered flask. ''Have some.'' He took a couple of gulps and passed it to me. ''You'll feel a lot more relaxed.''

I was scared. ''That's—I don't drink liquor,'' I said weakly.

''Who said anything about liquor? Would I give you liquor? It's just orange juice,'' he coaxed. ''Come on, have a swig. What *are* you—chicken?''

Just so he wouldn't think I was chicken, I took a sip. ''Ugh—that's terrible orange juice,'' I said. ''It's bitter.''

''But think of all that Vitamin C.'' Todd's voice was getting husky. ''Have some more.''

I didn't like the way it tasted, but I wanted Todd to like me, so I took a few more gulps.

Todd pulled me over closer and I shut my eyes. I had pictured it so differently:

> *Todd turned to Ellen as they strolled along the moonlit beach. Suddenly they stopped and looked at each other wordlessly. Then their lips met in a timeless embrace . . .*

''I said move over.'' Todd was jabbing at me. ''These seats are busting my buns.''

Before I even knew what was happening, Todd had grabbed me and was pushing me down on the seat, overpowering me with his muscular arms and the odor of those onion rings he'd just eaten.

''They don't call me Hot Toddy for nothing,'' he rasped. Instead of the timeless embrace I had dreamed about, it was more like being at the dentist's office with a suction device in my mouth. Only this was Todd's tongue.

"Please," I choked, trying to pull myself up. "I don't feel good. I think—that orange juice—it was—"

"Oh, come on." Todd gave a low laugh. "That wasn't plain orange juice. It was vodka and orange juice, otherwise known as a *screwdriver*."

A newspaper headline flashed before me:

RHODE ISLAND GIRL OVERCOME
BY FUMES

Hyannis, MA (AP)—Emergency technicians revived a fifteen-year-old mother's helper last night in a beach area known as Horny Acres. Her escort was quoted as saying, "Well, how should I know she was turning blue? It was too dark to tell."

Todd pulled me back. "Please," I cried, gasping for air, "I'm—"

"Wow," he said, "you're really turned on."

I wanted to tell him I was feeling terribly sick from the smell of onions and Todd's Old Spice cologne, which was a sickening combination. "Please stop," I begged.

"Now look." Todd's voice was harsh in the darkness. "I took you to a movie, I bought you something to eat. What'd you expect?"

He pushed me down again, locking his wet mouth on mine. New waves of onion fumes hit me. In slow motion, I could feel the Venus burger rising up . . . from my stomach to my chest . . . from my chest to my throat . . . from my throat to my mouth . . . and then . . .

"WHAT THE—" With a roar, Todd jumped away. He was yelling and swearing at the top of his lungs while waves of nausea erupted all over the front seat of his Camaro.

I tried to explain that it wasn't my fault, that I couldn't help it. But every time I opened my mouth, it was like Mount St. Helens erupting. All the while, Todd was swearing and hollering like a lunatic. *"YOU'LL PAY FOR THIS, YOU LITTLE . . ."*

Finally I stopped heaving. Todd was frantically wiping the steering wheel and the seat and his shirt, yanking Kleenex from the box of tissues on the dashboard.

All the while he kept screaming, "I'M GONNA KILL YOU FOR THIS."

Neither of us noticed the car door open. A bright light suddenly beamed into our eyes. It took a few seconds to realize there were two uniformed policemen practically blinding us with a flashlight.

"What the hell's going on here?" one of them asked.

23

I burst out crying and couldn't stop.

''What'd you do to her?'' the policeman demanded, yanking at Todd's arm.

''What did I do to *her*?'' Todd sounded hysterical. ''Look what she did to my car!''

''Girl got sick, Frank,'' the policeman told his partner. ''Probably drinking.''

''Buddy, you better clean that up fast,'' the one named Frank said. ''That stains.''

''Tell me about it,'' Todd said bitterly. ''I used up a whole box of Kleenex.''

The two police officers tried to question me but I was crying so hard I couldn't say a word.

They asked to see Todd's license and registration. ''Crowley,'' Frank said, peering at the driver's license. ''On Harbor Road. That's Ned Crowley's boy.''

''Him again?'' Frank's partner shook his head in disgust. ''I thought he looked familiar.'' Turning to me, he asked, ''How old are you, miss?''

''Fif—fif—fifteen,'' I managed to sob.

''Fifteen!'' Todd groaned. ''She told me seventeen.''

''Yeah, sure, Crowley. One of these days, you're gonna be in real deep trouble.'' Frank snapped off his flashlight. ''Don't let us catch you here again. Understand?''

"Wait!" I cried. "I don't want to ride home with him. I'm scared."

I jumped out of Todd's car and ran over to the policemen, still sobbing. Finally I was able to calm down and tell them where I was staying and that I worked for Martin Winner, the lawyer.

Just mentioning Mr. Winner's name made them a lot nicer to me.

"We'll take you back to the house," Frank said, and I hopped into the backseat of the police car. The last I saw of Todd he had taken off his shirt and was using it to wipe the dashboard.

I slunk down in the backseat feeling embarrassed, depressed, nervous—you name it. Once when I started to clear my throat, Frank pulled over quickly to the curb.

"Uh-oh. You getting sick again?"

I reassured them I was all right and scrunched down further into the seat.

So that was how I returned to the Winner house around 9:30 on Saturday night from my Big Date with Todd Crowley. My eyes were puffy and red, my dress was stained where I'd gotten sick, and I was limping because I'd broken the heel on my white sandals when I jumped out of Todd's car.

As we neared the house, I couldn't believe what I saw.

Not once all summer long had the family ever sat outside. But tonight—with my incredible good luck—everyone was out in full force, getting a breath of night air on the front porch. There was the Welcoming Committee—Mr. and Mrs. Winner, Marcie, Derek, and Grandma Brill. Standing on the sidewalk talking with them was Pete, back from his camping trip.

And good old Brandy Simms was sitting on the top step.

Frank's partner took my elbow and escorted me up to the house.

"It's Ellen!" Grandma Brill shrilled out. "In a police car!"

Everybody crowded around me. I could hear Marcie's voice asking loudly, "What happened? What did Ellen do?" She sounded thrilled.

The two policemen took Mr. Winner aside to reassure him. "Nothing to worry about . . . a little accident . . . she'll be all right . . . said she must have gotten sick from a hamburger . . . all over his car . . . ruined the upholstery . . ."

I wanted to disappear, to turn into vapor like the experiments in chemistry class. "You look awful," Marcie said as she danced off to turn on the porch light.

Pete came over to me and put his arm around my shoulder. "Don't worry," he said. "Everything's okay."

Like a jack-in-the-box, Brandy Simms had leaped up from the stairs. "What's going on?" she asked imperiously. "Where's Todd? He's supposed to take me to Sherri's party tonight."

"Tonight?" Pete asked. "Let me get this straight, Brandy. Are you saying Todd made plans to take you out to a party *after* his date with Ellen?"

"Why do you think I've been sitting around here?" Brandy said angrily. "Todd said he'd be back early. He was only going out with *her*. He was supposed to be back here by 9:15, and then we were going to go to Sherri's."

"I've got a hunch Todd's Camaro is a lot like Todd—pretty slippery." Pete sounded disgusted.

"Yeah—Ellen puked all over his car," Marcie broke into the conversation. "I heard the policemen telling my father."

"Oh, that's grotesque," Brandy said, her voice rising. "Why you miserable little . . ." she turned to me in fury. "It's all your fault—I can't walk into Sherri's party by myself! And you probably ruined Todd's Camaro!"

"Not to mention his reputation," Pete said.

I slept until noon Sunday morning and woke up with a terrible headache.

Then I remembered what had happened the night before and I didn't want to get out of bed. Ever.

There was a knock on the door. Before I could ask who it was, in came Marcie, carrying a cup and saucer.

"My mother said to bring you some tea. She wants to know how you're feeling."

"I think I have a virus," I lied, turning over and burying my face in the pillow.

"Okay, then—I'll drink it." The room was quiet except for the sound of Marcie slurping tea as she rocked in the chair. Downstairs the washing machine was humming, and Grandma was clanking dishes in the kitchen.

"Guess what?" Marcie said, "Todd's father came over this morning. Was he mad! He kept saying he was going to sue, but my father said something to him and he left."

Another knock at the door and in tiptoed Mrs. Winner. "How are you feeling, Ellen?" she asked. "Marcella, dearest, I need to talk to Ellen in private."

Marcie got up from the rocking chair grudgingly. She walked over to the door and just stood there, ears perked up like a little terrier.

"So, Ellen." Mrs. Winner settled herself into the chair. "Now, exactly *what* happened last night? I mean, did Todd actually *do* anything?"

Marcie crept closer to listen.

"He started to kiss me," I whispered miserably, "and I couldn't breathe and I got sick to my stomach."

"There isn't"—here Mrs. Winner gave a delicate cough—"anything you, er, left *out*, is there?"

"My mother washed your clothes from last night," Marcie informed me. "But there wasn't anything ripped or—"

"Sweetums, *please*!" Mrs. Winner looked pained. "It wasn't like that at all. I just thought I'd get some laundry done before we went out this afternoon."

If it wasn't so embarrassing, I would have laughed then and there. Did Mrs. Winner actually think that Todd had . . . that I had . . . that we had . . .

And furthermore, not once since I'd been there had I ever seen Mrs. Winner do a load of laundry—and certainly not *my* laundry. "All he did was kiss me," I said, tears starting up again.

Marcie giggled. "Pete said it must have been the Kiss of Death."

"That's quite enough, Marcella." Mrs. Winner stood up. "Well, Ellen, get some more sleep and you'll feel better. Go wash your face, Marcella—we're going out for a ride."

I had a hunch they'd probably end up at Sweet Tooth, but I didn't care. They actually left me alone all afternoon—and it was heaven.

I fixed two big peanut butter sandwiches and

brought them upstairs with a big glass of milk. Then I brought my radio into the bathroom and took a hot bath for nearly an hour.

I was back in bed, half asleep when I heard music. At first I thought Marcie had left the TV set on downstairs, but after a few minutes, I realized the music was coming from outside my window.

I could hear voices below asking, "What's going on," and a woman's voice saying, "Isn't that sweet!" I knelt by the window and lifted the shade to peer out.

I couldn't believe my eyes. There was Pete McIntyre in a bright green jacket, a big floppy hat with feathers like the three Musketeers wore, and a pair of shiny black boots. He was playing a guitar that caught the light of the afternoon sun. Next to Pete were the Mercer twins from across the street, plus their Saint Bernard dog, a young couple who always jog in the neighborhood, and a woman I never saw before.

Pete was singing *You've Got a Friend.*

There was a lump in my throat. Today of all days, it was exactly what I needed. A friend.

"Behold," Pete said, catching sight of me. "I have come to serenade the lady fair."

"Go for it, Romeo," said one of the Mercer twins, and his brother yelled, "Oh, Romeo, Romeo—wherefore art thou, Romeo." Everyone standing around began to applaud.

I pulled down the shade, feeling embarrassed. There were sounds of whistling and clapping from below. Then, a few seconds later, there was a tapping at the window. Again, I lifted the shade. There was Pete—perched in the branch of a tree, grinning at me.

"Fair maiden, I wouldst play a request for thee. What wouldst thou like to hear?"

"How about silence?" I said. We both started to laugh.

Pete shimmied down the tree, picked up his guitar from one of the twins, and started to sing again. By now some more people had gathered around.

"Milady needs her rest," Pete told them loudly. "She's had a weary road to travel. So let's all sing one last song to her."

He plunked a few chords on his guitar. "All together now—let's sing *You Are the Sunshine of My Life*."

They all looked up at me solemnly, like carolers at Christmas time.

They sang the song twice. There was a lump in my throat as I listened to them.

Pete bowed grandly. "Farewell, lovely lady," he called up to me. "Couldst thou give me a token of thy esteem? A handkerchief, perchance?"

I didn't have a handkerchief. All I had was a big clump of wadded-up tissues I had cried into the night before.

"Good night, sweet prince," I called down to him. "Parting is such sweet sorrow. This is all I have as a token. Pray, accept it."

The tissues went sailing down to where Pete stood, waving and smiling up at me.

24

"Everybody's talking about you!" Marcie reported happily. "They're all making jokes about Todd. Boy, is he mad at *you*."

I was a celebrity of sorts around Harbor Road, Marcie Winner had become a social butterfly. Just because I was still so humiliated over the Todd episode and wanted to lay low, suddenly Marcie wanted to go out. Everywhere.

"I'm sick of hanging around this house," she announced. "I wanna go out and *do* things."

She even wanted to go to the mall. Mrs. Winner was thrilled, figuring Marcie wanted to shop for school clothes. But I knew better.

Marcie was dying to see what would happen if I ran into Todd or Brandy.

I didn't want anybody to recognize me, so I wore my sunglasses and even borrowed one of those awful chiffon scarves from Grandma Brill to wear over my hair.

Just my luck, we ran into Mandy and Pam and their boyfriends in front of Waldenbooks. Even with my disguise, they spotted me. "Did you have fun last Saturday night, Ellen?" Mandy called out. I pretended I didn't hear her.

Later that day Marcie made a Big Announcement that stunned everybody.

I nearly cut my finger slicing a tomato for her

sandwich. "What did you say?" I couldn't believe my ears.

"I said I wanna go to the beach tomorrow. I betcha Pete would take us."

Mr. and Mrs. Winner were ecstatic when they heard. "I'm sure Pete won't mind driving you to the beach," Mrs. Winner said. I knew that was true. Earlier in the week, Pete asked me to go to Craigville Beach with him, but I'd told him no. I didn't want to see anybody from Lisa's crowd.

So, when Marcie suggested the beach, I pretended I had a cold so I could stay home. But Mrs. Winner insisted the sun would be the best thing for me. And Pete said yes, he'd drive us.

On Saturday morning around 11:30, Pete drove up in his father's Chevy.

"Because Marcie Winner is honoring us with her presence," he said, opening the car door, "because she is making her debut at the beach, I could not permit her to ride in my lowly pickup truck. Besides," he added, "my dad is doing a brake job on the truck today."

Marcie hopped into the front seat. She had even brought her own cooler, and she set it down, along with the towel, next to the window so I wouldn't be able to sit in front with them.

I climbed into the backseat with Derek. "Pete," I said, "don't you think it's kind of funny that Marcie wants to go to the beach all of a sudden?"

"I wonder if we'll see anybody there," Marcie said, settling herself down in the seat. "Suppose we see Toad? What do you think he'll say when he sees Ellen?"

"He won't say a word," Pete answered. "Todd wouldn't mess with me."

That made me feel better, like I was protected. For all my worrying, the day at the beach turned out to be very nice. None of Lisa's friends were there, so I was able to relax and enjoy myself.

Derek had the most fun. He loved the water. The two of us laughed and shrieked as we jumped the waves.

I chanted:

"Bobby Shaftoe's gone to sea,
Silver buckles on his knee . . .

Derek's lips were getting a little blue. I decided we'd had enough of the water, so we made our way back to the blanket, where Marcie and Pete were playing a game of gin rummy. "Oh, it's *you*," she said pointedly.

"You look like you're getting red," I told Marcie. "Maybe you should put your jacket on. And your hat, too."

"Oh, why don't you go haunt a horse," she retorted. I laughed and lay down on my towel to soak up the sun. It was a great day for getting a tan.

Marcie kept up a constant stream of complaints. The sun was too hot and the water was too cold. The sand was too sandy and her cooler didn't keep things cool enough.

The best part of the day was when she went in the water and a crab bit her toe.

That gave her something else to complain about on the way home. That and her sunburn.

"Look how red you are," I said. "You should have covered up like we told you. It was your first time at the beach."

"It's *your* fault," she said accusingly. "You

should of *made* me cover up. You should of insisted. A mother's helper is supposed to look after a little kid."

"Oh, poor baby," Pete said when he dropped us off in front of the house. "Poor, helpless little Marcie. Everyone picks on you, don't they?"

I was coming out of the shower when I heard Grandma Brill yelling that I had a phone call. I dried off quickly and ran to the phone. It was Pete.

"Listen," he said, "how'd you like to come over to my house tonight for a barbecue? I already checked with Grandma Brill and she said she's staying home tonight. So you haven't got any excuse to say no."

"A barbecue? Mmmmmmm. Sounds great," I said. "Are you sure your parents don't mind if I come?"

"Mind? Are you kidding? They're dying to meet you. They can't believe any mother's helper could last this long with Marcie."

The thought of meeting Pete's family sounded kind of nice. I didn't even feel nervous about it. As I started to get dressed, I automatically reached for my jeans. No, that wasn't right. The aqua sun dress I'd worn with Todd was hanging in the closet, freshly washed and ironed. Not that either.

Then I remembered the white pants Mom had gotten me before I left Pawtucket. They'd been a little tight then. But now they zipped up smooth as can be. I didn't even have to breathe in. Lisa had given me a brand-new green cotton sleeveless sweater with a V neck. The color was great now that I had a tan. It made my eyes look really green. I didn't want to wear the silver-and-turquoise earrings—they brought back bad memories. Instead, I put on a pair of gold hoop earrings Bobbie-Lou had given me for Christmas.

Marcie was sitting in the den watching television when Pete came by for me. Grandma Brill was putting vinegar on Marcie's bright red sunburn. "Vinegar takes the sting away," she explained. "Look what a terrible burn poor Marcie got."

As I expected, Marcie wasn't especially happy to see I was going out with Pete that night. "You must have put on a whole bottle of yucky perfume," she said. "You smell like a perfume factory."

"And you," Pete said with a glance at the vinegar bottle in Grandma's hand, "smell like a tossed salad."

He took my hand and we walked out the front door.

25

Pete's house was one of those big, comfortable, gray-shingled homes you see all over Cape Cod. Only even nicer.

There was an old-fashioned swing on the front lawn and a wishing well on the side of the house. Flowers hung over the wooden fence and burst out of the window boxes. What a nice place to grow up in, I thought.

We walked around to the backyard. Pete's mom came over and hugged me. "I'm so glad you could come, Ellen," she said. "Let me introduce you to everyone."

Mrs. McIntyre was a plump, pretty woman with hair the color of Pete's and the same blueberry-colored eyes.

"This is Anne, our oldest, and her husband, Jack. And those two little bandits," she said, pointing to the girl and boy racing around the yard, "are their twins, Jeff and Tracy."

Then there was Pete's other sister, Susan, who'd just graduated from Boston University, and her fiancé, Mark Hoffman. And Pete's brother Steve, who was a freshman at the university of Massachusetts. Plus a couple of other relatives. I was having trouble keeping everyone's name straight.

"Hey—how about me?" A heavyset man with thinning hair and a wide smile held his hand out to me. He was wearing a tall white chef's hat and an apron that said: ''NOBODY BAR-B-Q's LIKE I DO.''

''We wanted to save the best for last,'' Pete grinned. ''Ellen, this is my dad. And Dad—keep on flipping those burgers. We're starving.''

What a nice, friendly family they were. They had a way of throwing back their heads and laughing that made you feel like you were incredibly witty. Anne, the oldest, was really pretty. Susan had too many freckles, but still she was bubbly and cute. Even the twins were nice—they were off playing on the backyard gym set, not bothering anybody.

''Hope you don't mind getting thrown into all this,'' Pete said, leading me over to a big picnic table covered with a red-and-white plastic cloth. There were bowls of coleslaw and potato salad, and a platter of butter-and-sugar corn. My mouth started to water.

''Anytime you want to throw me into something like this, go right ahead,'' I whispered to Pete. ''It's like I died and went to heaven.''

Everyone sat down at the table. Pete's dad brought over a big plate of hamburgers and barbecued chicken. ''Come on now, people, dig in,'' he said. ''We've got a long way to go before we quit.''

Everything tasted wonderful. My appetite was extra good because I'd spent the day at the beach. Pete gestured at my empty plate. ''Hey, Mom—what did I tell you? Ever see a girl pack it away like Ellen does?''

Ordinarily, I might have been embarrassed by that remark. But with Pete's family, I felt so comfortable it didn't even bother me. They were always teasing each other and joking around.

"Pee-tuh," his sister Susan drawled, "you are such a male chauvinist. Apologize to Ellen. Right now."

"Okay, I apologize." He ladled some more potato salad onto my plate. "I guess with a job like Ellen's, she needs all the strength she can get."

"That's for sure," Susan agreed. "Remember the time I was a mother's helper for the Winners?" She started to laugh. "Marcie locked me in the upstairs bathroom and I couldn't get out. With my claustrophobia, I screamed my head off!"

Everybody laughed. They all knew about the Winner family, and especially about Marcie. "I remember when Anne baby-sat years back," Pete's mother said as she brought over a tray of brownies and refilled tall glasses of homemade iced tea.

"Marcie was a holy terror even back then," Anne recalled. "She wrote all over the living room walls in Magic Marker. Ellen, you should get some kind of medal to have lasted as long as you have."

After dinner, everyone helped clean up and then went into the living room to play games. I did really good because I love word games. We played Jeopardy and twenty questions and finally charades.

Pete announced that he wanted to act out a special charade. "This is in honor of Ellen," he said. "So don't anybody else try and guess. Let's see how smart she is."

He stood in the middle of the room, facing me. "To save time, this is a famous quotation. And this is the third word." He made a kind of flapping gesture.

"Wings!" I guessed. "Plane?" Pete shook his head.

"Fly? Flap? No—is it bird?" Pete shook his head yes.

"Okay," he called out, "second word." Anne complained that he wasn't supposed to talk. "Second word rhymes with this," Pete pointed to his nephew's curly blond hair.

"Boy?" I asked. "Curls?" Pete gestured that I was getting warm. "Curls—curly? You mean it rhymes with curly? Is it pearly? Girly? Early?"

"Early is right," Pete said. Everyone shushed him.

I was racking my brain. "Early. Bird. Something, something, early bird something." I leaped up from the chair shouting, "THE EARLY BIRD GETS THE WORM!"

Then I realized why Pete had given me that special charade. "Oh, you're rotten," I said, giving him a make-believe punch. But I couldn't help laughing.

Everyone wanted to know what the joke was all about, so Pete told them the story of my "worm-a-phobia" and the incident in the backyard with Derek and the worms. We all laughed hysterically.

We played a few more games and I couldn't believe the time. it was almost eleven o'clock and I knew I'd better get back to the house.

Everyone kissed me good-bye, and Pete's mom packed up some brownies for me. She told Pete he'd have to bring me back soon.

"For sure," I said, feeling happy. "And I won't let him *worm* his way out of it either."

When we got back to the Winner house, we sat in the car for a few minutes. Pete put his arm around me and we talked about a lot of things. I realized that this evening was the nicest time I'd had all summer long.

Pete brushed my hair back from my face. The

moon was bright and I could see him clearly as he smiled at me. "Ellen Jane Gardner," he said. "You're one fine lady."

He bent down and kissed me. There was the smell of honeysuckle in the warm August night and the sound of crickets chirping away.

I remember thinking how nice Pete's shirt smelled when I leaned my head on his shoulder—that nice, clean freshness when you dry clothes outdoors in the sunshine.

His mouth felt sweet and warm, and it was the most natural thing in the world for him to be kissing me, and for me to be kissing him back.

I learned something in that moment—that the real world can be more wonderful than any fantasy. Because Pete's kiss wasn't at all the way I had dreamed a kiss would be.

It was better. Oh, so much better!

The two of us walked up the front porch stairs slowly, arms around each other. "Good night, Ellen Jane Gardner," Pete said, kissing me again.

I never knew somebody could say my name and make it sound like a poem.

26

There's a certain time in August when you can practically smell fall in the air.

Grandma Brill must have sensed it, too. That morning at breakfast she started sniffling into her napkin. "Ellen, you'll be going back soon." Sniff. "It seems like you just . . ." Sniff. ". . . and soon it'll be time for you to leave . . ." Sniff.

"And good riddance," Marcie mumbled.

"Marcella—did you say *good riddance*?" Mrs. Winner sounded positively shocked—as if she'd never heard Marcie talk that way before.

"No—I said she's got good *rhythm*—you know." Marcie started snapping her fingers and shaking her shoulders.

"Now, now, sweetkins," Mrs. Winner said, not even looking up from her papers, "you're going to miss Ellen when she's gone. And Ellen will miss you, too."

"Ugh." Marcie grabbed her throat, making sounds like she was about to throw up. We all ignored her.

Although neither of us would admit it, we'd been having a pretty good time lately. Ever since Marcie decided to go to Craigville Beach, it was as if she was on a roll, making up for lost time. One day we took a day trip on the Woods Hole boat to Martha's Vineyard. Another time we went to the Glass

Museum in Sandwich. Pete took us to Nauset beach, and one time Lisa came along on a picnic at a state park.

We went to the library regularly now. Derek loved to pick out books and Marcie was even reading. Her taste changed from week to week. She switched from adventure stories to mysteries, then got into teen romances, believe it or not.

I took a walk with her and Derek to the drugstore to get *Seventeen's* ''Back to School'' issue. I was thinking about the clothes I needed for fall. Even though the day had warmed up and the sun was strong, you could sense that summer was winding down.

I had sneaked upstairs to my room to look through *Seventeen* when there was a knock at the door. It was Lisa. As soon as I saw her face, I could tell something was wrong. Especially since she had never come to my room.

Lisa sat down on the bed. ''Ellen,'' she said, ''I need to talk to somebody.''

This was getting interesting. ''Sure,'' I said, putting down the magazine. ''What's the matter?''

''It's about Jon. And me.''

Jon and Lisa? thoughts whirled through my head. Have they . . . is she . . .?

''Are you pregnant?'' I blurted out.

''Of course not!'' Lisa looked shocked. I felt kind of disappointed.

''If Father knew Jon was a hairdresser, he'd just die,'' she cried dramatically. ''He and Mother expect me to go with boys who want to be lawyers or doctors. Or maybe Accountants.'' Her eyes filled with tears. ''Mother always said she expected me to marry somebody who's successful. Financially, I mean.''

I thought about that a moment. "You know," I told Lisa, "the way I see it, if Jon is a good hairdresser, he can be just as successful as a lawyer. I mean, people always need a good haircut, but how often do they call a lawyer? Think about it."

But Lisa was still pacing the floor. Something else was bothering her. "That's not all, is it?" I said. Somehow I knew Lisa's deep dark secret.

"You want to be a hairdresser, too, don't you, Lisa?"

She whirled around and stared at me open mouthed. "Yes," she said in her whispery voice. "How did you know that?" Then she told me how she wanted to go to Wilfred Beauty Academy in Boston when she graduated high school.

"I don't want to go to college," she wailed. "But how can I ever tell Father?"

"Well, you don't have to say anything yet," I told her. "A lot of things can happen between now and when you graduate. Maybe next year if you still feel that way—"

"But what will I tell Father when the time comes?" Lisa asked piteously. "When it's time to apply to college—then what?"

"You can tell him about Mister Leo," I said. "Mister Leo is a hairdresser in Pawtucket, and he's so financially successful he could buy and sell all the lawyers there. And he has this big house and this boat and—"

I paused, stunned by what I had just said.

There was no such person as Mister Leo in Pawtucket. I had made it all up. It was something I did every once in a while—I made up these little stories to make people feel better. But I felt overwhelmed with guilt.

And then I felt something else—a sense of creativity. I had created a character, a fictional character. Lisa believed he existed. For a minute or two, I even believed he existed. *I wasn't a fabricator—or a liar—I was a writer!*

Lisa's face brightened and she threw her arms around me. "Oh, thank you, Ellen. I'll tell Father all about Mister Leo if he gives me any problems about Jon. Or about Wilfred Academy!"

She was so grateful that she wanted to give me something. I decided to take the bag from the "Rich Girls Store". It would be a good conversation piece at Pawtucket High.

It was chilly that night, so Mr. Winner decided it would be nice and cozy to light the fireplace in the family room.

If you didn't know better, it probably looked like a happy family scene. The fireplace was crackling away and in one corner the two little kids and their mother's helper were watching a horror movie on television. The beautiful teenage daughter was reclining on the couch, tweezing her eyebrows while her hair was being deep conditioned by hot oil under a special rubber cap. The two parents were busily talking business in the corner. And the friendly yard boy, Pete McIntyre, had stopped by and sat down on the rug next to the mother's helper.

From the kitchen came the smell of cookies baking. We could hear the familiar sound of Grandma Brill puttering around, banging cookie sheets.

The movie ended. Marcie flickered the remote control button and lay down on the braided rug.

"That wasn't so scary. The part where the kid turned into a vampire was dumb."

"Remember when you used to be a vampire, Marcie?" Pete teased. "You don't like going out in the daylight either."

Marcie liked being the center of attention. She pulled herself up from the floor slowly and held her hands as if they were claws. Then, hunching over, she made her way to Derek, dragging one leg.

"I am Vampira," she said, making slurping noises against Derek's neck. He stared at her in wide-eyed fright. "I will suck your blood, little boy."

Derek screamed and ran over to me. Mrs. Winner, still engrossed in conversation with her husband, didn't even turn around. "Don't carry on, Derek," she said. "Little boys aren't supposed to cry."

Marcie shrugged and stood up. "Hey, Grandma," she called out, "aren't those cookies done yet?" Poor Grandma Brill—Marcie had been nagging her all day to bake something called flim flams. They were supposed to be terrific.

Just then Mrs. Winner walked over to me with a yellow-lined pad in her hand. She had been making notes on it as she talked to Mr. Winner. "Oh, Ellen, dear, we've agreed we would like to have you return next summer."

She said it as if they had conferred the Nobel Prize on me.

"Uh, well, thanks," I managed to say. "But I don't know what my plans will be." I was saved by Grandma Brill.

"Here's the flim flams," Grandma Brill cried gaily as she carried a plate of cookies into the room. She set the plate on the coffee table. "I hope they're all right,'' she added a little anxiously. ''The way Marcie kept rushing me.''

Everybody ran over to get one. I took a bite of the still-warm cookie and stopped chewing. It was awful.

''Pooh! Yuck!'' Marcie spit out a mouthful of cookie. ''These are horrible. What'd you do to them?''

Mrs. Winner figured it out. ''You forgot the brown sugar, Mother.'' She sounded quite annoyed.

''Oh, my goodness . . .'' Grandma put her hand to her face. ''That's what it was.''

Marcie didn't take it lightly. She was furious. ''You ruined the flim flams,'' she shouted.

''I couldn't help it,'' Grandma Brill said in a small voice. ''I'm sorry.''

''My *other* grandmother doesn't ruin cookies!'' Marcie kept at it. ''Grandma *Winner* wouldn't forget the brown sugar! And *she* doesn't have a messy bedroom with papers all over the place. Who ever heard of an old lady with a messy bedroom?''

Pete had a tight, angry look on his face. As for me, I would have loved to smack Marcie then and there. I was tired of the way she was always comparing Grandma Brill with her other grandmother. According to Pete and Nedra, Mrs. Winner Senior lived in Arizona and hardly ever came to visit. She was too busy traveling.

From the corner of the room, Thelma Winner called out, ''Mother, stop bickering with Marcella. This is unacceptable.''

There was a buzzing in my ears. The way Mrs. Winner treated her own mother was awful. And Marcie was doing the same thing.

". . . And Grandma Winner doesn't have orange hair with dumb little bows in it. And *she* wouldn't forget to put sugar in the cookies. And besides," Marcie finished, "*she* doesn't have all those wrinkles in her face like *you* do!"

I looked at Grandma Brill standing there uncertainly with her "please-like-me" smile and the brave yellow bow in her hair. She looked like a small, wounded bird.

Nobody even came to her rescue. I was angry, angry at the people who hurt other people. And most of all, angry at the ones who just stand by and do nothing about it.

How, I wondered, could Mrs. Winner just sit there and let anyone talk that way to her own mother? She'd never let anyone talk that way to a client. For the hundredth time, I was grateful that my mom was the kind of mother who loved me enough to discipline me and teach me right from wrong.

The buzzing in my ears turned into a roar. "*Don't you dare talk that way to your grandmother again*," I yelled.

My hand reached out toward Marcie.

TEEN CHARGED IN ASSAULT

Ellen J. Gardner, fifteen, was indicted today for assaulting Marcella Winner, ten, who was described by her family as a shy, quiet child.

"This vicious attack on a defenseless little girl cannot go unpunished," vowed Martin Winner, prominent Cape Cod attorney, who . . .

Just in time, I caught myself and dropped my hand.

"*And furthermore*," I said, "*you apologize to Grandma Brill right now! And promise you will never ever talk that way to her again!*"

Out of the corner of my eye, I saw Martin Winner pull himself slowly up from his chair, as though he'd been stuck to it with Velcro. Behind his horn-rimmed reading glasses, his face was scarlet. "DON'T YOU *DARE* . . ." he cried in his commanding Bible-movie voice.

I could imagine what he was going to say. For sure they'd be sending me packing, back to Pawtucket.

But then I saw his finger pointing at Marcie.

". . . DON'T YOU *DARE* TALK THAT WAY TO YOUR GRANDMOTHER AGAIN," Mr. Winner said in a voice of wrath. "Ellen is right. You ought to be ashamed of yourself, Marcella. Apologize at once!"

Marcie's face turned the color of turkey breast at the deli counter. "I was only kidding," she said. "You don't have to get all huffy about it."

"APOLOGIZE!" Mr. Winner ordered.

"I'm sorry, Grandma." Marcie burst out crying and so did Grandma Brill.

For the next few minutes everyone pretended to be busy. Then Martin Winner broke the silence.

"Marcella," he said, "the fact is, your grandmother Winner never ever baked cookies in her life. Not even from a mix."

27

"I can't believe it's Ellen's last day," Grandma Brill sniffled as she scurried around the kitchen, her purple hair bow bobbing up and down. "I don't know where the summer *went* to this year."

We were getting ready for the Farewell Party in my honor. Actually, it was supposed to have been a Surprise Farewell Party. Except Lisa slipped and blurted out the big secret earlier when she asked if I'd have time to do some ironing before my Surprise Party started.

"Oh, you're so *dumb*, Lisa," Marcie said in disgust. "Why don't you go shopping for a new *brain*!"

Even though that Sunday was my last day, Mrs. Winner was not about to let me shirk my duties as mother's helper. "Oh, Ellen, dear," she reminded me, "don't forget to put in a load of white clothes after you set the dining room table."

I felt weird setting the table for my own Farewell Party. Still, I was impressed by Mrs. Winner's generosity. No expense had been spared. She had sprung for a paper tablecloth plus napkins, plates and cups that matched. I didn't even mind that they said "Happy Birthday."

"The children will miss you, Ellen," Grandma Brill dabbed at her eyes with her apron.

"And Ellen will miss them, too," Mrs. Winner said briskly.

I was in the laundry room, just about to put in a load of clothes, when Marcie stomped in.

"Are you really gonna miss me?" she wanted to know.

It was enough to make me nearly drop the basket of clothes. "Miss *you*? Are you serious?" I put my face close to hers and said, "Would I miss a wart . . . an abscessed tooth . . . a hemorrhoid? Would I—"

"Would you *please* brush your teeth," Marcie said, making a face as she backed away from me. "Ugh—your breath smells like eggs. I'm not gonna miss that egg breath of yours."

She started to chant: "Egg breath—smells like death . . . egg breath . . ."

I had to laugh. "Listen, Marcie," I said, "you better be nice or I won't tell you the exciting conclusion of *Murder in the Cranberry Bog*."

"Oh, *there* you are, Ellen," Lisa sang out as she waltzed into the laundry room. "I wanted to say good-bye and tell you I'm going to miss you."

"Oh, yeah," Marcie snickered. "You'll miss her ironing, that's what you'll miss."

"Ellen," Lisa said, ignoring Marcie, "I wanted to ask you something before you leave."

"Sure—what is it?" What could Lisa want to ask me? If I would write to her? If we could discuss her career plans? If she and Jon could drive to Pawtucket to visit me?

"I wanted to ask if you'd gotten a chance to iron my white dress," Lisa said.

At that, Marcie hooted. "Well, honestly," Lisa explained, "I *need* it for a party tonight."

I hadn't planned on doing ironing on my last day there, but, what the heck, I ironed Lisa's dress, which turned out to be a smart move. Lisa was so grateful that she gave me a brand-new leather pocketbook and a cotton sweater. I packed them into my suitcase quickly before she could change her mind.

We had an early lunch of frozen pizza—the kind you get in the supermarket. Around quarter of one, Pete came over. A few minutes later, the doorbell rang. In came Julienne and her husband, Tyrone, followed by Nedra, who was carrying a gaily wrapped package.

"We can't stay long," Julienne said. "We're on our way to my daughter's house." She gave me a hug. "Girl, you've done somethin' nobody ever done before. You lasted a whole summer as a Mother's Helper."

"Ellen is going into the Guinnesss Book of Records," Pete joked. "She sure left her mark on the Winner family."

"She sure left her mark on *you*!" Nedra shot back, and everybody laughed, including Pete.

We were talking and kidding around when Mr. Winner came downstairs and joined the party. As soon as he walked in the room, the whole atmosphere changed. Everyone fell silent.

Poor Mr. Winner—he can't help the way he is. That afternoon he was trying to be one of the guys, I suppose. But he didn't make it. I still break up when I think about his outfit—he was wearing *jeans*!

Rolled-up jeans, in fact, and a striped cotton T-shirt. Everyone stared at him. He looked like a hostage.

"Well, Ellen," Martin Winner said with forced heartiness, "how does it feel to be going back to Rhode Island?"

Was he *serious*? There weren't enough words in the English language to convey my joy. Luckily, I was spared having to answer because the doorbell rang. Derek ran to answer the door. In came Mom, wearing a denim skirt and a white cotton blouse. I ran over and hugged her and then I introduced her to Julienne's family.

"Oh, Laura," Grandma cried happily, giving Mom a kiss on the cheek. "Your timing is perfect. We're having a party for Ellen."

As she spoke, in came Marcie, carrying a big white bakery box.

"My mother got a cake for Ellen," Marcie announced. "It's from Bosworth's." Everybody murmured "ohhhhhh" because Bosworth's Bakery has the best cakes in town.

Grandma Brill pulled off the string, opened the box, lifted out the cake, and blinked.

The red lettering on the white frosted cake read: "HAPPY ANNIVERSARY BARBARA AND NICK."

"Oh, dear me," Mrs. Winner said with exaggerated surprise. "Why, imagine that—they must have given me the wrong cake. Oh, well."

Pete and Julienne exchanged a knowing look.

"Don't worry, Mrs. Winner," Pete said. "I'll bring the cake back. It won't take long."

"Oh, no, never mind," Thelma Winner said hurriedly. "It's not really that important. I mean—it's the thought that counts."

Julienne rolled her eyes to the ceiling and nudged Tyrone, who grinned broadly.

Then I realized what all the winking and grinning meant. Mrs. Winner hadn't ordered a cake for me at all. What happened was that Barbara and Nick must have had one big fight and canceled their anniversary cake. When things like that happen, you can pick up a cake really cheap at Bosworth's Bakery—which, incidentally, is a client of Winner and Winner's.

"Oh, who cares," Marcie said, licking her lips. "The ice cream's gonna melt. Let's eat." We all sat down at the dining room table, except for Mr. and Mrs. Winner who said they'd have their cake and ice cream a little later. They had been in a long discussion about some point of law and they wanted to look something up in the family room, where they kept most of their legal reference books.

There were some gifts piled next to my plate. There was a box of stationery from Julienne and Tyrone, earrings from Nedra, and the newest edition of *Writer's Market* from Grandma Brill. I hugged them and thanked them for my gifts.

There was also an envelope from Winner & Winner, P.C., Attorneys at Law. I couldn't believe it. Inside there was a check for $100 with a note that said: "Dear Ellen—a bonus for you. Hope you'll be back again next summer." The note was typed, with Lucy Bower's initials, all very businesslike.

There was even something for me from Marcie. "Don't open this now," she said, handing me a manila envelope. "Wait till you get to Rhode Island."

We were sitting there talking when suddenly Derek hopped off his chair and came over to me, holding his book of nursery rhymes.

"Oh, honey boy," Grandma Brill said, "Ellen can't read to you right now. The grown-ups are talking."

Derek shook his head and pointed to the picture on one of the pages. "Bobby Shaftoe," he said, clear as can be.

"Oh, Derek," I cried, delighted. "That's very good. You said that perfectly."

Derek glowed. He put the book on the table and gave me a radiant smile. And then he started to speak in a sweet, clear voice:

> ". . . Bobby Shaftoe's gone to sea
> silver buckles on his knee . . ."

You could hear a pin drop in that kitchen. There were goose bumps on my arms. Derek continued to recite:

> ". . . He'll come back and marry me
> Pretty Bobby Shaftoe."

"THELMA!" Grandma Brill jumped up, shrieking. "MARTIN! COME HERE—QUICK!"

From the family room, Mrs. Winner called out, "What is it *now*, Mother?"

"COME QUICK—IT'S DEREK!"

"'What *about* Derek?"

"He's—he's *blooming*!" Grandma Brill hollered.

Mr. and Mrs. Winner came racing into the kitchen and stopped still.

Rosy-cheeked, his brown eyes dancing, Derek was reciting the second verse:

> ". . . Bobby Shaftoe's fat and fair
> Combing down his yellow hair,
> He's my love forevermore
> Pretty Bobby Shaftoe."

Martin Winner stood transfixed. Mrs. Winner's mouth was gaping.

Grandma Brill broke the stunned silence. "Are you really, truly, talking, Derek?" she asked, looking confused. "Maybe he's just imitating sounds . . . you know, like a parakeet does . . ."

"I know Humpty-Dumpty, too, Grandma," Derek said shyly. He began to recite: "Humpty-Dumpty sat on a wall . . ."

Tears blinding my eyes, I jumped up and hugged Derek so hard he couldn't finish the nursery rhyme.

Mrs. Winner had regained her composure. "Well, Martin," she said, "I always told you Derek would talk when he was good and ready. Like I said, he was just a late bloomer."

"That's not it," Marcie said. "It was because Ellen was always reading to him all summer long." She looked at her brother with new respect. "Derek," she told him, "you speak really *good*."

Everyone started talking at the same time. If I stayed there another minute, I would have burst out crying.

"Pete," I whispered, "would you mind helping me get my things?" Pete followed me upstairs, his arm around me. Neither of us said a word. We got my suitcases and things and carried them outside to the car.

"Alone at last," Pete said. From his jeans pocket, he pulled out a little box, wrapped in white tissue paper, inside was a little gold heart on a chain.

"Oh, Pete," I said, "it's beautiful." I could feel the tears gathering again in my eyes.

"Hey, none of that," Pete said, taking my face in his hands.

He bent down and gave me a really long kiss. "This has to last till November," he said softly. "I figured if it's okay with your mom, I'd like to come to Pawtucket during Thanksgiving vacation to see you."

I started to feel a lump in my throat. As I said my good-byes, it grew.

"Ellen, honey," Mom said, "I don't want to rush you, but there's a lot of traffic today. We'd better get started soon."

Mrs. Winner clutched Mom's arm. "Laura, dear, as I was saying earlier, Ellen is welcome to come back again next year. Not as a mother's helper, of course. But maybe," she added archly, "now and then, she could, you know, sort of keep an eye on Marcella and Derek . . ."

"Ellen could get a job here on the Cape and stay with us," Mr. Winner said, making it sound like the Eleventh Commandment: *Thou shalt get a job here on the Cape and stay with us.*

Grandma Brill added the clincher. "And Ellen could go to the Cape Cod Writers' Conference next summer." She proceeded to tell Mom I had real writing talent.

There was a final round of hugging and kissing. "Don't forget to condition your hair every couple of months," Lisa said, giving me a peck on the cheek. Derek threw his arms around me, and I whispered, "Good-bye, Bobby Shaftoe."

Mrs. Winner kept urging Marcie to kiss me good-bye. "Oh, give it up," Marcie said loudly. "I'd sooner kiss a porcupine."

Then suddenly everyone left. Julienne, Nedra and Tyrone sped away in their Mercedes. The Winners went back into the house, leaving just

Pete. He gave me a quick good-bye kiss while Mom discreetly settled herself into the driver's seat.

He opened the door for me, then leaned his head in the window. "Say, Mrs. Gardner," he said to Mom, "got any more at home like her?"

"Nope," Mom said. "She's an original."

"Tell you what," Pete smiled. "I'll give you two camels, one donkey, three chickens, and some yellow beads for that girl. What do you say?"

"One more chicken and you might have had a deal," Mom laughed as she started up the car.

Somewhere along Route 195—I think it was right after Fall River—a funny feeling hit me.

Mom was talking about someone in her evening college class. I couldn't concentrate on what she was saying, because so many things were flashing through my mind, like scenes in a kaleidoscope—jumping the waves with Derek . . . Grandma Brill hopping around as she introduced me at the writer's group . . . Marcie's face when I caught her playing telephone pranks . . . the way Pete's strawberry-blond hair glinted in the sunshine as he waved good-bye to me on Harbor Road.

A whole bunch of feelings were crowding in on me. I wanted to hold on to all of them—the good ones and the not-so-good ones. They were all a part of me. And the way to save those memories was to put them into words. Maybe that's what real writing is all about.

It was a lot to think about. I leaned back against the seat and shut my eyes, ready for a really good daydream. It took a while because I was out of practice. I'd been so busy and happy the past couple of weeks, I hadn't needed any fantasies.

But still, it was good to know that whenever I needed them, my fantasies would be there—like the markers on Route 195—helping me get to wherever I wanted to go.

". . . And now—an interview with that world-famous writer, Ellen Jane Gardner," says the reporter. "Tell us, Miss Gardner, about the moment you knew for certain you would become a writer."

Ellen smiles reflectively as flashbulbs pop. "I remember it well," she says softly. "It was a Sunday afternoon in August on the way home from Cape Cod. I was fifteen years old at the time . . ."

"Oh, by the way, Ellen," Mom was saying, "what was in that envelope Marcie gave you?"

I reached over for the manila envelope on the backseat. "Well, at least it's not ticking," I said, holding it up to my ear.

There was a folded piece of white bond paper inside. I opened it up and read the words Marcie had so carefully printed in purple Magic Marker:

ROSES ARE RED,
VIOLETS ARE BLUE,
A DONKEY'S A JACKASS
AND SO ARE YOU.

"Oh, did she make you a little farewell card?" Mom asked, glancing briefly at the purple printing. "That was nice of her."

"Very nice," I said, perfectly straight-faced. "It's the kind of thing you'd expect from Marcie Winner."

For some reaons, I felt a lot better after I read the card. I put it back carefully in the manila envelope. I wanted to show it to Pete when he came to Pawtucket over the Thanksgiving vacation.